COWGIRL ON THE RUN

QUEENS OF MONTANA, BOOK 4

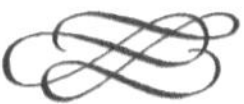

VANESSA GRAY BARTAL

DRY CREEK PRESS

CHAPTER 1

Sixteen-year-old Maggie Chapman heard hooves pounding in the yard and knew it could only be her best friend, Mathew Henshaw. She smiled at her reflection in the mirror and flew down the stairs to greet him.

He gave her a radiant smile when she opened the door and stepped out onto the porch.

"Hey, baby girl," he said. He swept her up into a tight hug.

"Hey, Mathew," she said, and returned his hug. He was such a sweetheart, she thought. She enjoyed the easy affection of their relationship. Her sister, Kitty, was on the porch, but she slipped inside when Mathew started to talk. Maggie sometimes wondered if her sister secretly disliked Mathew. She was always running off whenever he showed up. That didn't seem likely, though. Everyone everywhere liked Mathew. He was sweet and adorable.

"What's that smile for?" he asked.

"I'm thinking how great you are," she told him. "The best friend ever."

His smile faltered. She wondered why. Maybe he was shy about compliments. Lately whenever she told him how much she appreciated him or what a great friend he was, he got that same look, like he found her words painful. Maggie didn't understand, but that was nothing new. It seemed like she was always the last to know everything, and then she usually only found out because Kitty told her.

Her older sister was whip-smart and a keen observer of people. She knew everything about everything, and Maggie had a hard time not envying her. It had been Kitty who told her their oldest sister, Anne, was falling in love with Will and he with her. And then a couple of years later, Kitty told her Dobbie was falling in love with Libby, and Libby with Dobbie. Now both couples were getting married this summer. Maggie sighed wistfully. Would she ever meet her Prince Charming and fall in love?

"You're distracted today," Mathew said.

She blinked at him and shook her head to clear it. "Is that unusual from any other day?" She was a dreamer. Most people thought she daydreamed about the animals she loved, and she did do that a lot. More often than not, however, she dreamed of her future and the unknown man who would someday sweep her off her feet. She was sixteen and had never been kissed, an embarrassing fact she kept to herself. At times she looked at Mathew and debated with herself about asking him to teach her. But then she would shake her head and blush at her forward thoughts. He would most likely be mortified and upset at the disruption in their pleasant friendship.

They spent the day as they usually did, in the woods looking for animals, watching the clouds, and talking. There was no one on earth she was more comfortable with than Mathew. He had been her best friend for as long as she could remember. They had played together as often as they could all through her growing up years, only parting when there was work to be done or school to attend. He was the one who had to work or attend school, however. She was home-schooled because there was no one to take her, and her family spared her from working on the ranch, a fact which secretly annoyed her. Why was everyone but her allowed to pull her weight? The only time she ever felt like she was helping was when Libby asked her to pick berries or work in the garden, but any little girl could do that.

Mathew stayed for supper as he almost always did. He was two years older and had graduated high school a couple of weeks ago. Ever since his graduation he stayed at their ranch from sun up to sun down. Maggie was surprised because she had assumed he would start working full time on his family's ranch. When she asked him about it, though, he became annoyed.

"They don't need me," he said irritably. "And they give me meaningless tasks to complete, like I'm a baby."

"I know exactly what you mean," she said. She felt the same way.

He smiled. "I know you do."

His smile did something strange to her heart, and it started to pound unnaturally. She cleared her throat and looked away. "I wonder where Kitty is today." Her sister disappeared shortly after Mathew's arrival.

"Dunno," Mathew said carelessly. He kicked the step lightly with his boot.

Maggie studied him. "Don't you like Kitty?" He and Kitty were the same age. Maggie had always wondered if they would someday get together.

Mathew gave her an odd look as if the question surprised him. "Sure I do. She's your sister."

"That was a strange thing to say."

"I suppose you would think so," Mathew said.

Maggie's frown deepened. She had the sense Mathew was withholding something from her. "Is everything all right?"

His face cleared, and his smile looked genuine. "Right as rain."

They were standing on the porch. Maggie stood on the step above him so they were eye to eye because he was much taller than her five feet and four inches. As she looked at him he looked at her, and the air between them suddenly felt strange and heavy. His hand rose, as if to touch her, and then the door behind her opened.

She turned to see Kitty exiting with a man, a very handsome man who was tall with dark hair and dark eyes. Maggie's heart beat faster, and then the guy said her name.

"Maggie!" He sounded astonished. "How are you?"

It took her a minute to place him. "Dante? Oh my goodness."

Dante was their neighbor from across the street. He had moved when his parents divorced, and she hadn't seen him in years. She jumped into his embrace and hugged him tightly.

"Look at you all grown up," he said. "You were only ten years old when I went away, and still in pigtails." He tugged lightly on her hair.

Maggie felt an odd stirring she had never felt before. Dante was everything she had ever dreamed when she pictured her perfect prince: tall, dark, and handsome.

Beside her Mathew cleared his throat. "Hi, Dante."

Maggie turned to look at him. He sounded strange, hostile, even. She had never heard him use that tone with anyone. Why wouldn't he like Dante? His strange behavior continued when he put his arm around her waist. She blinked up at him in surprise.

They made small talk for a few minutes and Maggie's brief hopes about Dante vanished. It was obvious even to her he only had eyes for Kitty. He put his arm around her and called her "my girl." Of course he would like Kitty. She was smart and beautiful with her curly chestnut-colored hair and interesting brown-green eyes. Maggie's hair was dishwater blond, and her plain brown eyes were far too large for her face, she thought.

Mathew was silent as they watched Dante and Kitty walk to the barn.

"I can't believe he's back," Maggie said.

"Hmm," Mathew answered.

"He's changed. Remember when he left he was short and chubby?"

"Yes, I remember distinctly. I'm surprised you do. You were only ten when he went away," Mathew added, but Maggie wondered if that was originally what he meant. Mathew was certainly acting strangely, she thought.

His odd behavior continued when they entered the house. He sat beside her, but he seemed preoccupied. He didn't talk, although he did put his arm around her and absently run his fingers through her hair.

Kitty entered looking flustered and embarrassed. She never liked to be the center of attention, and now the family was pelting her with questions about Dante.

Maggie decided to add her two cents and see if she could smoke her sister out. Kitty almost never gave her own opinion on things, and Maggie could never tell what she was thinking or feeling.

"He's really cute," she said. Kitty's blush deepened. She didn't comment, but Mathew did.

"He seemed standoffish," Mathew said.

Maggie's head whipped around to look at him in surprise. Where was all this venom coming from? He studiously avoided her eyes by keeping his gaze fastened on Kitty.

Maggie faced forward, fists clenched. Why was he staring at Kitty with such intensity? Did he like Kitty? Despite the fact that she had harbored a secret hope that he and Kitty might one day get together, now that the possibility of Mathew being attracted to her sister was staring her in the face, she found herself uncomfortable. If Mathew was with Kitty, he would spend all his time with her. Maggie would be left out and lonely.

She realized Kitty was crawling into her shell and trying to be demure about Dante. Suddenly it was very important to her that her sister continue whatever was developing between her and Dante.

"But you're going to see him again, right?" Maggie blurted.

Mathew looked at her and scowled, confirming her suspicion. He obviously wanted Kitty and didn't want Dante in the way.

Maggie didn't want to alienate Mathew if he truly had feelings for Kitty. She leaned toward him and rested her head against him.

She felt him relax and draw in a breath.

"Come with me," he said. The note of command in his tone was unusual. He was usually the embodiment of sweetness and gentleness with her. He took her hand and led her outside so abruptly she had to sprint to keep up with him.

When they reached his truck he stopped short and then spun to face her. He opened his mouth, closed it, and then opened it again.

"Mathew is something wrong?" she asked tentatively.

"I," he started, and then stopped again. "I should go. Bye." He jumped into his truck and left her standing there, puzzling over his odd behavior with a frown on her face.

CHAPTER 2

The next morning he showed up at his usual time. Unlike usual he was remote and out of sorts. In all her sixteen years she had never known him to be grumpy. His behavior was troubling to her.

Add to that Dante's reappearance that morning, and she had much to puzzle over. She had never been good at figuring things out, and her head swam with all she was trying to keep straight. Mathew was acting strangely. That was one fact. Dante was here, and he seemed to like Kitty. That was fact number two. Kitty was flushed and embarrassed, more so than usual. Maggie wasn't sure if that was significant information, but it was possible Dante was having that effect on her. She determined to keep an eye on all three of them. Maybe by observing their odd behavior she could figure out what was going on.

She sighed with the hopelessness of it all. Without Kitty to explain things to her she was sure she would never understand, and she couldn't ask Kitty because Kitty was too private to betray her own thoughts and feelings.

She didn't realize she was staring at Kitty and Dante until Mathew spoke.

"You really think he's nice looking?"

She glanced at Dante again. She had taken a step back now that she knew he was Kitty's, but even from an impersonal point of view, Dante was handsome.

"Yes," she said.

Mathew muttered something to himself. She couldn't be sure, but it sounded like, "Now or never, Henshaw."

He stood abruptly and held out his hand to her. "You're coming with me."

She smiled at him. The command was so unlike him it amused her. "Am I being taken prisoner?"

He didn't answer. Instead he grasped her hand and dragged her behind him.

"Where are we going?" she asked.

"You'll see," he threw over his shoulder.

She trotted along behind him, turning her head to watch the scenery as they passed. It really was a beautiful day, she thought.

"Did you see that baby chipmunk?" she asked when they finally stopped.

"No. Do you remember this?" He stepped aside so she could see behind him.

He had taken her to the woods, and she did recognize what he was indicating. It was a fort they built several years ago when she was ten.

She smiled. "I can't believe it's still standing."

"I make sure of it," Mathew said. "I check on it often, but that's not the point. The point is we built this together. It's something that's ours. When we built it, I used to pretend it was our house. That we were married and this was where we lived."

Her cheeks pinked, and she looked at him in surprise. "You did?"

He nodded. "I came back one day after we stopped playing here and I did this." He took her hand to tug her forward.

She leaned close to see what he was pointing at. "M.H. and M.C." She straightened. "You carved our initials in our fort?"

He nodded, looking nervous. She wanted to soothe him, so she reached out her hand and rested it on his forearm.

"What's this about?" she asked gently.

"I love you," he blurted. "I've loved you as long as I can remember. I've never wanted anyone but you. If you don't want me in return then we'll go on being friends, but I can't go another day without you understanding the truth of what I feel for you."

Her head was swimming. Mathew was in love with her? How had she missed that? What did she feel for him? Certainly she loved him, but was she in love with him?

"Mathew, I," she started, but he put his finger to her lips.

"Let me do this before you say anything." He leaned toward her and gave her a sweet, lingering kiss on the lips. The kiss finished, and they parted slowly. She kept her eyes closed, and then she smiled. Her hands snaked between them and grasped his shirt. Something profound had happened to her in that moment their lips met. Something sweet and beautiful blossomed inside her, like a rosebud opening its bloom.

She opened her eyes and looked up into his hopeful, worried eyes. "Who else but you?" she whispered. "You're everything."

He let out a breath and almost sagged with relief. When his hands snaked around her they were shaking.

He kissed her again, and she practically melted into the warmth and comfort of his embrace. She had to turn off her mind because it was suddenly exploding with new information. Everything in her life seemed to line up and fall in place like dominoes. This was why Mathew acted the way he did; he was in love with her. This was what it felt like to be in love. This was what her sisters, Anne and Libby, experienced that made them smile and stare at nothing every time their fiancés were around. And perhaps the biggest realization of all: this was the man she was going to marry. She was correct in what she told him. Who else but him? He truly was her everything—her best friend, and now her love.

"Look what else I found," he said when the kiss was finished. He tugged her hand toward the little shack again.

She leaned in to look. Next to her initials were two other sets of initials. "E.C. and S.D., and A.C. and W.A.," she read out loud. "My sisters carved their initials in our fort?"

Mathew shook his head. "I asked. Dobbie and Will did it."

She smiled beatifically. "I think our fort might be magic."

"It is for us," he said. "It will always be ours. I'll keep up on it, and someday our kids will play here."

She hugged him and rested her head on his chest. "Our kids," she repeated. The thought wasn't surprising or alarming to her. Maybe in some hidden part of her brain she had always known she and Mathew would end up together.

He led her inside the small building.

"This felt larger when I was ten," she said.

"It feels right to me," he said. They were pressed tightly together in the small space. He took her face in his hands and kissed her again.

"I love you," he breathed.

She smiled against his lips. "I get that now. Sorry it took me so long. I'm not very good at figuring things out." She wondered if anyone knew of his feelings, and if so she wondered why no one told her.

"You're perfect," he told her sincerely.

She smiled at him and slipped her arms around his neck. He genuinely believed she was, and she knew it. Of course she wasn't, but she knew Mathew would always view her that way.

"We're lucky," she told him. She wasn't wise or worldly, but she knew some people searched their whole lives and never found half of what she and Mathew had together, or what they would always have together.

"Blessed," he amended.

"Blessed," she echoed, and this time she kissed him.

CHAPTER 3

*T*wo years later...

*I*t was her eighteenth birthday, and Maggie's head popped off the pillow with purpose. She supposed some people might not like knowing when they were going to get engaged, but Mathew had told her from the beginning of their relationship two years ago that on her eighteenth birthday he was going to propose.

"Happy birthday, sweetheart," her sister, Libby, said when Maggie descended the stairs and entered the kitchen. She came over to hug her and give her a kiss on the cheek.

Maggie smiled and returned her hug with enthusiasm. Libby lived in her own house since she married Dobbie. Usually Kitty cooked breakfast now, or they ate cold cereal. Having Libby cook for them again was a special treat for her birthday.

"You look happy today," Libby said.

"And that's so unusual from any other day," Kitty said.

Maggie looked at her in confusion. "You don't think I'm happy on most days?"

"I was being sarcastic," Kitty said. Maggie never understood her when she used sarcasm. "The sun should be as happy as you are."

Maggie giggled. Kitty and Libby smiled at her, and then Libby returned to her breakfast preparations. Maggie sat next to Kitty who immediately motioned for her to lean close. Maggie did, and pressed her ear close to Kitty's mouth.

"Did you notice?" her sister asked.

"Notice what?" Maggie whispered.

Kitty pointed to Libby. Maggie turned to study her. She didn't notice anything out of the ordinary, but that was nothing new. She wasn't observant, and on the rare occasions she was she couldn't make sense of her observations. Without Kitty or Mathew to explain things to her she would stumble blindly through life, totally unaware of her surroundings. It was a fact of her life she did not enjoy.

"I think she's pregnant," Kitty whispered.

Maggie gasped and Kitty placed her hand over Maggie's mouth.

"I don't think she knows yet," Kitty said. "I don't think we should be the ones to inform her."

Maggie nodded and Kitty removed her hand.

This has to be the best birthday ever, Maggie thought. A baby! Her heart sang with the new information. She tried to picture a baby who would resemble both Libby and Dobbie; two of the people she loved most in the world. She would spoil it. She would adore it. She would devote her life to it until she had a baby of her own, which hopefully wouldn't be very long. Mathew promised they would be married in less than a year and he said they could start trying for children as soon as they were married. He was as anxious for kids as she was.

"Have you heard from Steve lately?" Kitty asked. Her sharp tone worked to draw Maggie out of her happy daydreams.

"No," she said. Libby set a plate of pancakes in front of her along with fresh blueberry syrup. Maggie beamed at her before drowning her pancakes in syrup.

"Nothing?" Kitty persisted. "No letters, no phone calls, no personal confrontations?"

"No, Kitty." She paused. "Oh, wait. He sent me a letter."

Kitty sighed in exasperation. "I want to see it. Did you keep it?"

Maggie shook her head. "I threw it away."

"When?"

Maggie tried not to sigh. She wanted to eat her birthday pancakes in peace. "Yesterday."

"Maggie, I told you to tell me if you received any more communication from him," Kitty said reproachfully.

"I forgot," Maggie said.

Kitty let out a frustrated growl. "I'm going to go dig through your trash to get the note."

"Okay," Maggie said. She returned to her pancakes with relish as soon as Kitty disappeared, but her peace was disrupted by her sister's return.

"Maggie," she said sharply.

Maggie jumped and looked at her.

"How could you not tell me about this?" She shook the letter for emphasis.

Maggie loved her sister, truly she did. But she was a criminal justice major who had a couple brushes with vigilantism in years past. She fancied herself as the female Marshall Matt Dillon of their community. Maggie smiled at her own witticism. She wasn't usually able to think of things like that.

"This is not funny," Kitty said.

Maggie's smile faded. "I'm not laughing at that," she said. "No offense, Kitty, but I think you're overreacting. Steve has some sort of crush on me. Mr. Henshaw talked to him about it, and he promised to back off."

"Maggie," Kitty said in the exasperated tone Maggie was accustomed to. The two sisters were very different, and sometimes those differences made Kitty crazy. "This is not some sort of crush. This is crazy." She shook the letter again. "I'm taking this to the sheriff today, and I'm going to talk to him about a restraining order."

"No, Kitty, you can't." Maggie's eyes turned round and her tone was pleading. "It would be embarrassing, and he might get in trouble."

"He deserves to get in trouble," Kitty practically yelled.

"Mathew doesn't think he's dangerous," Maggie said.

"Mathew is as sweet and innocent as you are."

Maggie's eyes filled with tears. Kitty's tone gentled. "That's not an insult. It's a compliment. You're a rare treasure in a cynical world, both of you. I love you both, but this is serious, and I can't let it slide any longer. Did you read this letter?"

Maggie blushed faintly. "No. I opened it, saw it was from Steve, and threw it away."

Kitty fought hard to maintain her temper and patience. She wanted to shake some sense into her baby sister. "Listen and I mean really listen, don't daydream while I'm talking."

Her sister knew her well. She forced her mind to focus on Kitty's words.

"*Dearest Maggie*," she started. "*Only a little while longer until we can be together. I can hardly sleep at night for thinking of how you'll feel beside me. I can see you, smell you, taste you all the time now, and it's maddening. I know you have to pretend not to see me. I know things are complicated for us, but I'm about to simplify them, and I know you'll thank me. We'll be together again soon, darling girl. Until then, know that I am yours and you are mine.*"

Kitty set aside the letter and looked up. Maggie was pale and blinking rapidly. "What does he mean we'll be together again?" she asked. "We were never together. He knows I'm with Mathew."

"That's what I've been trying to tell you," Kitty said patiently. "He's delusional. He's sick in the head. He thinks you're in love with him. No amount of talking will convince him otherwise. He is twenty-five years old, and he's been obsessed with you since he started working for the Henshaws almost two years ago. This has gone on long enough and I'm going to do something about it. Today. This very minute, in fact." She stood.

"All right," Maggie capitulated. "I can see something needs to be done to stop him. He's obviously unstable if he thinks I could ever be interested in him, but do you have to do it today on my birthday?"

Kitty started to open her mouth, but Maggie rushed on.

"Tomorrow," Maggie said. "Wait one day, please, Kitty. That can't possibly hurt anything. I want to enjoy this day with no stress. It's a very special day." She smiled a secret smile.

Kitty smiled in return. She loved her sweet, clueless little sister. She knew Maggie thought no one knew Mathew was set to propose today, but neither Maggie nor her boyfriend had ever been able to keep a secret. Everyone in the Chapman family as well as the Henshaw family knew what was coming.

"All right," Kitty said. "But promise me you'll be very careful and very aware of everything today."

Maggie bobbed her head in an enthusiastic nod.

Kitty would have Mathew make the same promise, for all the good it would do. Together they were possibly the two sweetest and most innocent people in the entire world.

CHAPTER 4

"There's my girl."

Maggie had been so absorbed in her conversation with Kitty she hadn't heard Mathew enter the house. Now she pushed aside her pancakes and flew into his arms.

"Mathew," she exclaimed. She gave him a smacking kiss on the lips.

"Happy birthday," he said.

"I'm eighteen," she said significantly.

"Yes, I know," he said. He wagged his eyebrows at her and she giggled.

"I'll leave you two alone now," Kitty said.

Maggie had forgotten her sister was there.

"Remember what I said, Maggie," Kitty added before she left. "Be careful."

Maggie nodded absently.

"What did that mean?" Mathew asked. He sat, pulled Maggie into his lap and started to feed pancakes to her.

"I got a letter from Steve," she said after she swallowed her bite of food.

Mathew froze. "You did? When?"

"Yesterday. Kitty wants to go to the sheriff and request a restraining order."

"Maybe that's for the best," Mathew said after a pause. "He's been a good worker for Dad, but this is getting out of hand, especially after he agreed to back off when Dad confronted him a couple of weeks ago."

"What did your dad say?" Maggie asked.

"He told him you and I were together and getting married. He made it clear it was unwise for an employee to be hitting on his employer's future daughter-in-law."

Maggie's cheeks pinked with pleasure. She loved Mathew's parents, and it pleased her her future father-in-law had defended her so. "That's nice," she said.

"Isn't it, though?" He squeezed her gently, and then nuzzled her ear with his nose and kissed her neck. "Missed you."

"Missed you, too," she whispered. It had only been a few hours since she last saw him, but any separation felt agonizing. They got lost looking in each other's eyes for a few minutes.

"Are you finished with your pancakes?" he asked.

"Are you asking because you're ready to go or because you want to eat my leftovers?"

"Both," he said.

"I'm finished."

He reached around her to quickly eat the remainder of her food and then he stood.

"What are we doing today?" she asked.

"It's a surprise." He took her hand and wove their fingers together.

First he took her to the barn. He coaxed her up the ladder and into the hayloft.

"My very first memory when I was three years old happened right here in this very spot," he said. "Mom brought me and Marcus over for a play date, but she didn't trust us not to wreak havoc on your family's property. She and your Mom sat in the barn and talked while we played. I climbed up here to spy on everyone, which was very adventurous because I was a little guy, and I maneuvered the ladder all by myself. I remember peering down at you, sitting in your mom's lap. You were one and not walking yet, and you liked to be held all the time. I hadn't really paid much attention to you up to that point, but that day you looked up and noticed me. We looked at each other and you laughed. I remember feeling proud of myself I made you laugh, and I remember thinking maybe babies weren't so bad. I started to hide and pop my face out and you laughed hysterically. You laughed so hard my mom turned to look and I got in trouble for climbing up into the hayloft by myself."

She smiled, pleased by his story. "I'm sorry I got you in trouble."

He pulled her into his arms. "It was worth it." He touched her face lovingly. "You're my first memory, Maggie." He leaned in to kiss her, and she responded by putting her arms around him and pulling him as close as she could.

"Ready?" he asked when the kiss ended.

Her face puckered. "We're not staying here?"

"Don't tempt me, or you're going to get me in trouble again."

"Oh." Her face colored, and she smiled demurely. They hadn't gone farther than kissing because they wanted to wait until their wedding night. Or at least Maggie did.

They descended the ladder. He took her hand again and led her to a nearby bullpen. He pressed her against a fencepost and put his arms on either side of her.

"One day when I was eight and you were six, we were standing right here watching the new bull being unloaded when he broke free and gored Rex. Do you remember?"

She nodded. It was the first time she ever saw someone injured, and it was traumatizing so soon after her mother's death.

"You turned and threw yourself into my arms and my heart stopped. You asked me to tell you when it was over, but I didn't because I didn't want to let you go. Marcus saw and teased me about it later, but when he realized I didn't care he said, 'You really like Maggie, don't you?' And I said, 'No, I love her.' It was the first time I said it out loud, but the feeling never wavered." He kissed her. Once again she wasn't ready for him to let her go when he did.

Next he led her to his truck.

"I didn't think we had any memories in here," she said.

"Sure we do," he said. He winked at her, smiling when she blushed. "But that wasn't why I brought you here. When you were twelve and I was fourteen I went home one day and told my mother I was going to marry you. She said, 'Sure you are, honey.' I thought she was patronizing me and I got angry with her. She took me to the closet, opened it, and showed me this."

He reached to the seat behind her and handed her a silver plate. Inscribed on the top of it was "Mathew and Margaret Henshaw."

"She told me she would fill in the date of our marriage at the bottom," Mathew said.

This time she kissed him, and with enthusiasm, although his truck was parked in the middle of their yard and there were cowhands milling by.

"Maybe we should go someplace more private," he suggested when he could find a pause between her kisses.

He took her hand and led her into the woods. As they got farther in she realized he was taking her to their old fort, and her heart started to pound with anticipation.

When they arrived she noted a faint glow emanating from the small building. On closer inspection there were about a dozen candles scattered in and around the small building, and what looked like dozens of white roses strewn everywhere.

Maggie gasped.

Mathew turned toward her and took both her hands in his. "This is the spot where two years ago my life really started. The happiest day of my life was when I kissed you and you told me you love me, but I think today might be able to top it."

He got down on one knee and pulled a small box from his pocket.

"Maggie, you are my life, my very breath. Will you marry me?"

"Yes," she whispered. Tears had started coursing down her cheeks as soon as he opened his mouth. He slipped the ring on her finger and stood to kiss her. "I love you," she whispered.

He took her hand and led her into the fort and then gathered up all the roses and piled them in her lap while she laughed helplessly.

"You're burying me," she said.

"I'm showering you. There's a difference."

She laughed delightedly, storing away memories to tell their children. When he at last had all the roses piled in or near her lap, he sat down beside her.

"That was fun," he said.

"It was the best," she said.

He sat up excitedly. "Maybe we should carve our kids' initials in the wall."

"We should probably have them first," she said.

"Come on, we already know what their names are going to be. It will be fun to bring them here and tell them about how we got engaged and then show them their initials."

She smiled uncertainly and looked at the wall. It would be fun, but something held her back. She wasn't usually a pessimist, but she had the disturbing feeling that if they did it they might never get the kids they wanted. "Let's wait until they're born," she suggested.

"All right," he agreed. "We'll wait until they're actually here. Speaking of which, let's talk dates. If we set our wedding for October that gives us four months. Is that enough time to plan?"

"With Libby leading the way all things are possible," she told him. Libby was good at planning events.

"My mom and Libby working together could take over the world."

"I'm not sure Libby would need your mom's help, but it will be fun to let them have at it."

He put his arms around her. "Did I tell you I love you, future Mrs. Henshaw?"

"Yes, you did, future Mr. Henshaw."

"I'm already Mr. Henshaw," he pointed out.

"It's not official until we're married," she said. She tipped her face up for a kiss, and then opened her eyes to look at him in confusion when the kiss ended abruptly.

He was lying in her lap unconscious and behind him stood Steve with a log upraised over Mathew's still form.

CHAPTER 5

*H*er first reaction was a blood-curdling scream.

"Come on," Steve said. He held out a hand to her.

She stared at him, and then turned her attention to the still form in front of her. "Mathew." She shook him gently. "Mathew."

"Come on," Steve said more impatiently.

"No," she said, not sparing him a glance. "What have you done?" She shook Mathew again, but he didn't stir. Blood trickled from the back of his head and she pressed her hand to it.

"I made it so we could be together, but we have to hurry. We don't have a lot of time until he comes to." He held out his hand to her again.

She shook her head. Tears poured down her cheeks. "I'm not going anywhere with you."

"You can stop pretending now, he can't hear you," Steve said.

There was so much madness in his voice she finally looked up at him. "What?"

"I know you've been keeping up appearances with him until we can be together. You're legal now and we can get married without your dad's permission, but we have to hurry."

"I'm not going anywhere with you." Her voice sounded small and afraid, even to her own ears.

Steve glowered. "Maggie, I don't like disobedience. Come with me now, or I'll kill him." He poked Mathew's unconscious form with the toe of his boot and raised the log again.

"No," Maggie screamed. She jumped up. "All right, I'll come with you. Leave Mathew alone."

He hesitated, and she wondered if he was thinking of finishing Mathew off anyway.

"I-I want to go," she stammered.

His smile was more like a grimace and his eyes gleamed with something that terrified her. How had she missed his insanity before now?

"All right," he said happily. He took her hand to lead her behind him, and she tried hard to repress her shudder of revulsion. Bile rose in the back of her throat, but he was oblivious as he dragged her behind him at a trot. At first she thought he was muttering something, but then she realized he was singing an upbeat song.

Think, she commanded herself. She forced her eyes to her surroundings. If there was one thing in her favor it was her familiarity with the land; it had to be better than his. Or so she thought until she realized he was leading her to the Henshaw's property with a purpose. The Henshaw's spread was so vast even some of their most seasoned cowboys occasionally became lost, but Steve seemed to know exactly where he was going. He had dropped the stick he used to hit Mathew. Maggie debated picking up her own stick to use on him, but decided against it. Like most cowboys she knew, he was large and well-muscled. In a fight he would overpower her without effort, and she didn't want to be at his mercy physically. No, her best bet was to keep him calm while she tried to think of a plan.

She wished she had a cell phone. She had never wished for one before because most of the time they were useless, but on the Henshaw's property she could get a signal and call for help. Belatedly she thought she should have taken Mathew's, but she had never used a cell phone before, and she would prefer for Mathew to be able to call for help when he came to. *If he came to.* No, she wouldn't allow herself to think that.

They walked for what felt like an hour. They skirted the edge of the Henshaw's property, so she was familiar with their location the entire time. She debated making a run for it into the deeper recesses of the woods, but if he caught her, he wouldn't be happy. At least now she knew where she was, and they seemed to be heading toward the road. Even if there were no other cars nearby she might have more of a chance at being observed with him.

A twig snapped behind her. Absently she turned, expecting to see a fawn or woodchuck, but instead she caught sight of Mathew as he ducked behind a tree.

Steve froze and listened.

"Did you see that deer?" she asked, hoping her lie sounded convincing.

He turned and scanned the horizon behind them. His eyes were narrowed, calculating. "A deer? I don't see it."

"It bounded toward the east," she said. Her voice shook, and she swallowed hard. "They're so fast; much faster than elk, don't you think?"

His eyes focused on her and roamed her face. She forced herself to smile, even though her lower lip quivered.

He nodded. "That's so, but elk meat tastes better. After we're married I'll go hunting and get us some elk for the winter."

She should probably tell him she liked that idea, but she couldn't bring herself to do it. She was barely able to hold back her panic, so she didn't think she should push the little act she was putting on for his benefit. At least Mathew was alive, and he was following them. He would use his phone to call for help, she was sure of it.

Her hand shook in Steve's, and she worked to make it stop. When Mathew was unconscious she had the peace of mind that he was out of harm's way. If Steve saw him…She shook her head. Mathew was tall and strong, but he was no match for this madman.

Go away, Mathew, she silently commanded. Stop following us. Get help.

Panic and exertion were making her mouth dry. She concentrated on the feeling in order to ignore the other feelings trying to break free inside her. She was going to die, and she knew it. At some point she would have to try and get free, and then he would kill her.

As long as Mathew is safe, she repeated to herself until it became a mantra. Protecting him was her new number one priority. She didn't allow herself to think about the fact that protecting her was most likely Mathew's top priority. *God, please don't let him do anything foolish,* she prayed. Like her, Mathew wasn't one for critical thinking. He was impulsive, and he would do the first thing that occurred to him if he thought it might save her.

Abruptly they reached the road and she jerked to a halt. There was a truck sitting before them; a truck she had never seen before.

"This doesn't belong to the Henshaws," she said.

"It's mine," he said proudly. "I bet you didn't know I already had a car for us, but I do. I've been planning our future for a long time."

"Wh-where are we going?" she asked.

"Wyoming or New Mexico. There's always work to be done on a ranch. I figure Mr. Henshaw will give me a good recommendation, and I can get a job as foreman."

The fact that he had bashed his boss's son in the head and still thought he would get a good recommendation was a sign of how deep his lunacy went. Still, Maggie was in a hurry to get in the truck with him before Mathew could reach them. He would have to stop for gasoline at some point, and she would try to make her escape then. There was no way she wanted to risk an altercation that might get Mathew injured. Or worse.

She opened the truck door without waiting for him to do so and jumped inside. Steve grinned at her and then hopped in his own side.

"Anxious, aren't we?" he asked.

She nodded and stared straight ahead, trying to force down the vomit working its way up her throat.

"All right, honey, let's go," he said merrily. He started the truck. Some part of her brain noted it needed a new muffler because it rumbled loudly. She thought they were making a clean get away but Mathew jogged into the clearing behind them.

Don't look back, she silently pled with Steve. At first she thought he didn't see Mathew because the truck accelerated forward. Then she watched with horror as he spun the truck around. Too late she realized he had been increasing the distance so he could gain speed.

"Don't," she screamed. Her voice tore from the strength of her emotion. "Steve, please don't. Leave him alone."

But it was too late. Mathew turned and started to run away, but there was nowhere to go. The truck hit him with such impact that his body flew up into the air and landed on the hood.

"Stop screaming," Steve said. His tone was conversational and held no emotion.

But Maggie couldn't stop screaming. In fact, it was all she could do. Mathew rolled off the hood and onto the pavement. The truck turned again, and he pressed the accelerator to the floor. A minute later an elk stepped into the roadway and Steve slammed on his brakes with an uttered curse.

All at once Maggie's mind came back into focus. She had to get to Mathew. She had to help him. As soon as the truck slowed enough for her to jump out, she put her fingers on the handle and jerked. She bounced and rolled a couple of times as she flew from the vehicle, but she didn't feel it.

Mathew was lying in the roadway, crumpled and unmoving. She must have reached him in record time, but she didn't care. All that mattered was helping him, saving him. Behind her the door of the truck opened and Steve stepped out.

"Maggie, leave him be. He's nothing to do with us now. Come on, honey, our wedding is waiting." When she didn't stop or turn toward him he instantly became enraged. "I don't want to have to punish you on our wedding day, but I will."

She ignored him and dove to Mathew's side. He was blinking slowly and blood trickled from the side of his mouth. She gathered him in her embrace.

"It's all right," she told him. "It's all right. You're going to be okay. We're on your property. Your dad can fly you to the hospital."

She didn't know if he could hear her, but he seemed to look at her with recognition because he smiled a little half smile.

"Mathew, stay with me," she pled. "Please, stay with me."

But he didn't. She had watched the life seep out of too many animals not to recognize what was happening to him.

"No," she screamed frantically. "No, don't leave me."

He blinked once, again, and then no more. The life drained from his eyes and left him staring blankly toward the sky.

CHAPTER 6

*S*ome corner of her mind comprehended the rumble of trucks, but she didn't look up. She continued to hold Mathew, pleading with him to come back to her.

"I'll be back for you soon, honey," Steve said. "I'll never let you go. Remember, Maggie. You're mine."

A door slammed and a truck started, but she didn't look up.

"No." The grief in Marcus Henshaw's voice matched her own, and she did look up when he knelt across from her. "What happened to him?"

"He...he hit him with his truck," Maggie said. The voice didn't sound like hers, and she still couldn't believe the words were true. Marcus looked over her shoulder with hate-filled, narrowed eyes. He yelled something behind him and she realized her father and Dobbie were there, along with several of their ranch hands and a number of the Henshaw's cowboys. Mathew must have called both families, or they called each other. A couple of trucks took off in the direction Steve had headed.

Her father approached and knelt beside her. "Marcus, do you have your phone?" She had never heard her father's tone so gentle before, and she looked at him in wonder. Reality was fading and the lines of her vision were becoming blurry. "We'll need to call the sheriff."

Marcus fished in his pocket with shaking hands and gave his phone to Maggie's father. He stepped away a few paces and spoke urgently into the phone.

Marcus and Maggie stared at each other across Mathew's body with a look of, "What now?"

It was an endless moment of shared grief and confusion, broken only by the return of her father.

"Let go," he said in the same gentle tone he had used earlier. She didn't know he was talking to her until he touched her hands and attempted to pry them off Mathew.

"No," she said. She clutched Mathew closer.

"Maggie, honey, you have to let go now. He's gone."

"No." She had never screamed at her father in defiance before, but he didn't seem to mind that she did it now. "He could come back. He's going to come back to me." The rational portion of her brain knew she was making no sense, but her fractured emotions were in control now.

Her dad looked at Marcus for help, but Marcus was staring blankly at them, and Mathew Chapman must have realized he would be no help. He signaled to a couple of their ranch hands and they knelt to flank Maggie.

"We're taking you home now," her father spoke in the voice he used to tame a spooked horse.

"No!" she screamed again. "No, no, no, no, no!" She clutched Mathew's shirt in her hands, and when the two ranch hands peeled them off, she fought them as she had never fought anyone.

Of course it was a losing battle. Even the old and wiry cowboy Rook was too strong for her. They half carried, half dragged her to her father's truck and then held her still on the long drive to her house.

By the time they arrived home she was more than subdued, she was catatonic. Her father easily lifted her and carried her into the house. Libby and Kitty were both waiting to ask him questions, but he ignored them and carried Maggie to her room.

He sat on her bed and ran a gentle hand over her hair. A part of her brain noted the action with surprise; her father wasn't known for being affectionate, but she was too far gone to truly process anything. Finally she felt sleep claim her and sank into the bliss of oblivion.

When she woke it was dark and Kitty was sitting in a chair beside her bed. She sat forward and laid a hand on Maggie's arm.

"Can I get you anything?"

Maggie shook her head. "What happened after I left?"

Kitty studied her, debating if she should tell her. Anyone else probably wouldn't, but Kitty was more comfortable with facts than emotions.

"The sheriff arrived. They took a statement from everyone at the scene. He left a form for you to fill out when you're ready. They issued a description of Steve and his truck. The Henshaw's men weren't able to catch up with him."

"What h-happened to M-Mathew?" She had to force herself to say the words.

Kitty took a deep breath and tried to steady herself. "The county coroner arrived and took him to be autopsied. The funeral is day after tomorrow. The Henshaws decided against a viewing."

Maggie nodded. She didn't want a viewing, either. "How are they?"

"Mr. Henshaw seems all right. He and Marcus are shaken, but you know how men are."

"And Lydia?" Maggie asked. Lydia Henshaw was Mathew's mother.

"Not well," Kitty said. "She's under sedation at her house."

Maggie nodded. There was silence for a minute until she couldn't take it anymore. "It's all my fault, isn't it, Kitty? If I had listened to you, if I had reported him this wouldn't have happened."

Kitty crawled in beside her and hugged her tightly. "No, you can't think that way, Maggie. He is sick in the head. Even if we reported him he might have found a way around the restraining order. I was worried, but even I didn't think he would ever go to this extreme.

There is no way any of us could have seen this coming, and there is no way it's your fault."

Maggie nodded, but she didn't believe her sister. It was her fault, and no one would be able to convince her otherwise. After all, it was Steve's strange obsession with *her* that had killed Mathew. If she had done more to discourage him or paid better attention to his strange behavior, Mathew would still be alive; she knew it.

"Want me to stay with you?" Kitty asked.

Maggie had to think about that. She would need to be strong eventually, but not tonight. "Yes," she choked.

Kitty nodded. She stood and walked to the chair, and when she returned, Maggie saw the flash of a gun. Kitty checked the safety and then rested it on the nightstand beside her head. Kitty had received a handgun for her eighteenth birthday. She was an excellent shot, and Maggie had no doubts her sister would shoot anyone in order to protect her.

"You think he'll try again, don't you?" Maggie asked.

"I have no doubts whatsoever," Kitty said resolutely.

Maggie shuddered. If he came in through the window Kitty would have the drop on him, but if he somehow entered the house and sneaked in through the door he might overtake both of them.

"Dobbie's sleeping outside the door with a shotgun," Kitty said. She put her arms around Maggie again. "Don't worry, Maggie. We're not going to let anything happen to you. We're all going to protect you, no matter what."

Instead of feeling reassured Maggie felt panicked. He would keep coming for her; she was certain. Who would he kill next in his pursuit of her? Kitty? Dobbie? Her father? Libby and her unborn baby?

The tears started then, and they weren't simply tears of fear. Her grief for Mathew overwhelmed her. Kitty held her as she cried for the next two hours, and then they both fell into a restless sleep.

CHAPTER 7

The funeral was a nightmare. She and Lydia Henshaw alternately clung to each other and their other loved ones. Kitty and Libby flanked Maggie and tried to support her during the day, but it didn't work; she was insupportable.

As she physically deteriorated, her father and Dobbie took over. They escorted her back to the house and carried her inside before taking up their posts on guard. In addition to her deep grief she felt nervous and on edge, imagining Steve around every corner. It helped that Kitty arrived soon after and never left her side. She stuck to Maggie like glue, even waiting outside the bathroom when it became necessary. And she always had her gun on her, strapped to her side in a holster her boyfriend, Dante, had bought her for Christmas.

"This must be the most unromantic gift ever," Dante had complained when he presented it to her.

"Not to me," Kitty said, her eyes shining with excitement.

Strange that Maggie should remember the scene now. She barely registered it at the time.

For the next few hours after the funeral, she slept with Kitty by her side. It was dark outside when Kitty shook her awake.

"Maggie, wake up."

Maggie sat up in alarm. "What? What is it? What's happening?"

"Nothing. Everything is fine, but the sheriff is downstairs. He has some information I think you need to hear."

"All right." She drew herself slowly out of bed and followed Kitty unsteadily down the stairs.

When they arrived at the base of the stairs almost everyone in the room turned to frown at them.

"I don't think Maggie should be a part of this." Their father, Matt Chapman, expressed what everyone in attendance was feeling.

Maggie looked around at Libby, Dobbie, Dante, her father, and the sheriff.

"I do," Kitty said. "She needs to understand everything and, at this point, sheltering her isn't going to do any good. She needs to know what's going on. She needs to know what we're up against." She turned to Maggie. "Do you want to stay, or do you want to go back upstairs? I'll go with you if you want to leave."

Maggie surveyed the room. She had the feeling what she was about to hear would change her forever. No longer would she be the innocent, carefree little girl who played in the woods all day. Although even as she thought it, she realized Mathew's death had already seen to that. Her childhood was over. She was a woman now.

"I'll stay," she said. She sat beside Dante, and Kitty sat on her other side.

The sheriff drew in a deep breath. "First of all, let me say how sorry I am, Maggie. I know you've been through a traumatic ordeal. I wish there was some way I could go back and prevent that. Short of that, I can promise you we'll do our best to catch him, but it may be more difficult than I first thought."

"What do you mean?" Maggie asked. Her mind felt foggy. She worked to make it focus.

"Since the event I've been doing some looking into Steve Fenton's background. Let me tell you I was amazed at what I found." He took another deep breath, clearly unwilling to proceed. Maggie hoped he wouldn't make her beg for the information. Kitty was right; she needed to know everything about her attacker. Finally the sheriff continued unprompted.

"Steve joined the army when he was seventeen. He became a ranger. I'm not sure if you're familiar with them, but they're Special Forces. Only the most elite are invited to join. His career was going well until he was involved in some sort of conflict; I don't know what, it's classified, but after that he was let go on medical disability. My guess is that means he went nuts and got kicked out. Anyway, I wouldn't know what I'm about to tell you if I didn't have a buddy high up in the army, and even he had trouble finding out, but Steve was involved with covert operations. He spied on people, and he had extensive wilderness training."

"Wh-what does that mean?" Maggie asked uncertainly. She vaguely knew what he was hinting at, but she needed it spelled for her. Kitty, like usual, explained things in a way she could understand.

"It means he can tap our phones. He can listen to our conversations. He can watch us when we don't know he's here. He'll know where we are at all times. He'll know when you're alone. He'll know how to get to you."

"Y-you can't be serious," Maggie stammered. She searched the faces around her. They looked grave and worn, and it was more than grief making them that way. They were worried.

"There's more," Kitty started.

"I don't think…" her father started, but Kitty interrupted him.

"Dad, she's not a baby any more. If you try to protect her from the truth it might get her killed," Kitty said.

Her father shuddered and nodded curtly.

Kitty clutched Maggie's hand. "He bragged to one of Henshaw's men that he stood in your bedroom and watched you sleep a few times. The cowboy laughed it off as idiotic bragging because he thought it was impossible for someone to sneak in here, but since everything has come to light, we think it's true."

Maggie shivered convulsively. She wanted to throw up. He had been in her room? He had watched her sleep?

"Why didn't he kill me then and save Mathew?" she burst out.

Everyone looked at her in surprise.

"I don't think he wants to kill you," the sheriff said slowly.

"Death would be a better alternative than what he has planned for me," Maggie said. Everyone was still looking at her in astonishment. She closed her eyes and turned her head away.

Conversation began to swirl around her, but she tuned them out. They were planning strategy and setting up shifts to guard her.

"What about your aunt?" Dante said quietly. "Your mother's sister."

Maggie's stomach dropped out. Was he really suggesting she go live with her unknown aunt in New York City? She couldn't leave Montana. She was a country girl, through and through. She would die being shut up in a dirty, crowded city.

"No," Libby said vehemently. "We barely know her, and what we know of her we don't like. Maggie can't go that far from home, especially now when she needs us the most." She started to cry. Dobbie put an arm around her and pressed a gentle hand to her stomach. *He must know about the baby*, Maggie thought.

And that was what did it. "I'll go," she said.

All eyes were suddenly on her.

"What? No. You can't." They all voiced their dissent at once, but she held up a hand. Seeing Dobbie lay a protective hand over his unborn child made her realize she had to do some protecting of her own.

"You can't guard me every minute. It's exhausting and stressful. Kitty's going back to college in a few weeks. Dante's starting his new job. Dad and Dobbie have work to do on the ranch." *And Libby is going to start showing any day now.* "Going away is the best solution all around. I'll be out of harm's way, and the sheriff will be free to look for him without worrying about my safety."

"But…" more than one of them started. She held up her hand again.

"I won't hear any argument. I'm going, and that's final." She pressed her lips together in what appeared to be a resolute line. In reality she was trying hard to stop them from trembling.

CHAPTER 8

aggie sat on a bench and tried not to cry. For two
months she had lived in New York City, and for every
minute of those two months she had been in abject misery. Besides
grieving for Mathew, she had her aunt to contend with, and things
between them weren't going well.

She was five when she met her mother's only sister. She remembered her the way she thought of a fairy princess: pretty, glossy, and
not quite real. There had only been that one meeting when her aunt
came to visit Maggie's mother as she neared her deathbed. Maggie
always thought it was sad they didn't have more of a relationship with
her mother's only living relative. Despite her grief, she had hoped to
get to know her and learn something of the mother she only dimly
remembered.

Now what she knew of her aunt she wished she could take back.
Her first words to Maggie had been critical, and nothing since had
mellowed the atmosphere between them.

"Is that what kids wear in Montana these days?" she had asked as
she inspected Maggie's jeans and t-shirt.

Maggie hadn't even looked at herself after her aunt's comment.
She usually had what she believed to be a savvy fashion sense, but in

the days following Mathew's death, she was concerned more with survival than clothing.

"The first thing we're going to have to do is enroll you in high school," her aunt said as soon as the clothing remark settled.

Maggie did respond to that. "I already graduated."

Her aunt, Victoria, rolled her eyes. "You were homeschooled in some backwoods fashion. That hardly counts."

"I had an online curriculum, and I also had a tutor for a while," Maggie said.

Her aunt sighed dramatically. "I suppose that will have to do, although you'll never get into a decent college with such a lackluster education."

"I don't want to go to college," Maggie said.

Victoria stopped and stared at her. "Then what do you intend to do with your life?"

Maggie's eyes filled with tears. For the last few years she had planned to get married and have children. Beyond that she had no idea. Maybe her aunt was being harsh with her because she was unaware of the circumstances that brought her here. Maybe she should fill her in.

"My fiancé was murdered," she said quietly.

Victoria rolled her eyes and shook her head again. "Fiancé." She threw out the word like it was a disease. "Really, what is your father thinking letting you get engaged at such a ridiculous age? Most people I know don't even begin to think about marriage until their thirtieth birthday. It's impossible for someone of your age to truly be in love. I didn't get married until I was thirty five."

And now you're divorced, Maggie thought bitterly, but she didn't say it. No one in her life had ever talked to her the way her aunt was now talking to her. It was a bitter pill to go from the care and comfort of her home where everyone pampered and petted her to her aunt who couldn't bring herself to say one kind word to her niece.

Since her arrival two months ago, her aunt had sniped and snapped at her until Maggie thought she might go insane; but she couldn't defend herself because in reality she was dependent on her aunt for her very survival. She had nowhere else to go.

Worse than her aunt's criticism was Maggie's own stifling loneliness. It was the first time she had ever been away from home. Now she was thousands of miles away, living with a relative who seemingly detested her, and unable to contact her family in any way. It was the one thing they grudgingly agreed on before her departure: No contact. Since they had no idea if Steve was watching them, they didn't want to risk alerting him to Maggie's whereabouts. As long as there was no contact, she was perfectly safe.

She didn't feel safe, though. She felt vulnerable, scared, and alone, and the feelings were made worse by her new city. It was huge. It was bustling. Everyone was in a hurry all the time. The only reason she left her aunt's apartment at all was to escape the woman's incessant attacks.

But because she was too afraid to venture more than few blocks for fear of getting lost or being attacked, she hadn't seen much of the city. The one highlight of her new existence was Central Park. Her aunt lived on the Upper West side of Manhattan, only five blocks from the park. It was at the absolute edge of Maggie's comfort zone, but she came every day, rain or shine, and sat on the same park bench. She stared unseeingly at the beauty around her and took some small comfort in nature, mostly because it had always been a source of comfort to her, and she had nothing else.

Far away she heard the clip-clop of hooves and thought she must be dreaming. Lately she had some trouble distinguishing reality from fantasy because she talked to no one and spent all her time alone in her grief-filled world. She was slowly but surely going crazy, and proof of that fact now stood in front of her because she was staring into the sweet face of a beautiful horse. When she blinked at it to clear her vision, it didn't go away. Her eyes swam with tears. It was such a strange and poignant reminder of home she was overwhelmed.

A person slid off the horse's back and sat gently on the bench beside her.

"Are you all right, Miss?" a heavily accented voice asked.

Maggie looked at the man, barely registered his police badge, then burst into tears and propelled herself onto his chest.

*N*ick Marino had never experienced anything like what was happening to him now, and that was saying a lot. After three years on the force in two different precincts, he thought he had seen it all. He was wrong.

He was ambling through the park on one last tour before he signed off for the day when he saw her. A girl sat on a park bench, looking more lost and alone than anyone he had ever seen. Right away he knew she wasn't a local, and he wondered if she was a tourist in need of help. When he approached she looked up at his horse, and Nick drew in a breath. She was beautiful; possibly the most beautiful girl he had ever seen. It wasn't that she was physically nice looking; pretty girls were a dime a dozen where everyone was trying to make it as an actress. No, there was something more to her, something in her face that drew him in and left him breathless. Although she was clearly sad and upset there was still a sweet, soft innocence in her eyes and around her mouth. He had never encountered anyone with that look before, which was why he dismounted his horse. Usually when he confronted someone who might be in trouble he stayed on his horse to maintain a sense of detached authority. This girl wouldn't allow detachment, though. He had to be near her to make sure she was okay.

Still when he sat and asked about her wellbeing, the last thing he expected was for her to throw herself into his arms and weep. That had never happened to him before, and he wasn't sure how to respond. In the end, he decided to turn off his law enforcement instincts and do what came naturally as a man. He enfolded her in his embrace and drew her tight against his chest.

As he did so, he had the strangest sense he had been handed responsibility for her, as if she needed a keeper and some unknown hand elected him. He shook his head as if to clear it. That was crazy. What woman in America today needed a man to look out for her?

True, he watched over his girl cousins and female friends in his neighborhood, but he did it quietly and without their knowing. Goodness forbid he should trample their independence.

As he held her and allowed her to weep on his chest, a delicious sense of belonging crept over him. He had dated more than his fair share of women, but none of them had ever felt this good in his arms, and wasn't that a kick in the teeth. Was he losing his mind? He was a police officer on duty, and he was holding a strange tourist in his arms. Professionalism took over when common sense failed, and he gently pushed her away from him so he could see her face. Her hair was long and more blond than brown. If she had on any makeup it was long gone after her many tears, but she didn't need it. Her complexion was flawless, especially with her cheeks rosy after crying. Her eyes were a soft brown and the largest he had ever seen in such a tiny face. They would have overwhelmed the rest of her if not for her full, pouty lips. What would it be like to kiss those lips, he wondered, before giving himself another mental lashing.

"Miss, may I help you in some way?"

She shook her head and pressed her fingers to her eyes to try and stop the flow of tears. As she did so he noticed a diamond on her left hand and his heart sank. He didn't see a band, and his many female cousins had spent so much time talking about rings he knew that meant she probably wasn't married.

"May I take you back to your fiancé? Have you become separated?"

She nodded, and then shook her head. "My fiancé is dead," she blurted, and her tears started anew.

"Oh," he said, angry with himself for dredging up her pain. "I'm sorry. Was it recent?"

She nodded. "He was m-murdered."

He froze with his hands gripping her biceps. "Here?" He racked his brain for recent homicides in the city. There were too many to decipher which might be her fiancé.

She shook her head. "In Montana."

"Montana?"

"It's a long story," she said.

"People tell me I'm a good listener," he said. "Like my horse. I sit here and don't say a word."

She smiled faintly at the reference to his horse. "I didn't expect to see a thoroughbred quarter horse in the middle of New York City."

"I didn't expect to see someone who knows what a thoroughbred quarter horse is in New York City," he said, and her smile widened before it slipped.

"You don't have to talk about it if you don't want to," he added.

"The truth is I would love to talk about it," she said. "I have no one to talk to. I'm not certain I should burden a stranger with my story."

"I'm not a stranger; I'm a policeman. We're duty bound to help in any way we can. You need someone to talk to; I'm here to listen."

"All right," she said quietly. And then she told him a strange, sad, and frankly scary tale. He was used to dealing with victims who weren't always as innocent as they seemed, but for some reason he bought her story completely. She was guileless and incapable of making up such a horrific tale.

"I'm sorry, Miss," he said when she finished. "I'm truly sorry for your loss." And he was. His job had made him cynical, but there was only sincerity in his tone when he spoke to her. She was clearly undeserving of the misfortune that had befallen her. His horse whinnied and Nick checked his watch.

"I'm off duty," he noted absently.

"Oh," she said. Her tone rang with a disappointment that made his heart sing. She was sad to see him go, and that pleased him, even if all she wanted from him was a listening ear.

"It doesn't sound like you've seen much of the city," he commented.

She shook her head. She reached her hand to pet his horse's muzzle and smiled when the horse leaned in to her touch.

"I have an idea," he said. "Why don't I take you out tonight and show you a little of what you're missing here? Lots of people fall in love with New York, and I think if you gave it a chance you could be one of them."

"I don't know," she said hesitantly. She wanted to go, but he was a stranger.

"I'll take you back to the stable with me and you can see the rest of the horses."

Her face lit like he had offered her a million dollars and he smiled, too.

"Really?" she asked in an awed whisper.

He nodded. "You can help me curry my horse, if you want." He would have to slip the stable manager a ten for the favor, but it would be worth it to keep that smile on her face, he thought.

"All right," she said. She stood to her feet and bobbed excitedly.

"Unfortunately I can't let you ride my horse, and it's a long walk back to the precinct building."

"Not a problem," she assured him. "If there's one thing country girls are accustomed to it's walking."

He smiled at her. It took everything within him not to walk beside her and put his arm around her. He had no doubt how that would look to passersby who expected their police officers to look cool and professional, so with a repressed sigh he swung up into the saddle.

She put a hand on his shin to stop him. "What's your name?"

"Nick," he said. "Nick Marino." He held out his hand for her to shake. "What's yours?"

"Maggie Chapman."

He smiled. She smiled. And that was the exact moment he lost his heart.

CHAPTER 9

The walk to the precinct building was long. Maggie had no idea the park was so vast. She amused herself on the way by imagining what Kitty would say if she could see her now.

You met a stranger on a horse and you're following him who knows where for who knows what?

She could picture the look on her sister's face, and it wouldn't change if Maggie tried to defend herself.

He's a police officer, and I have a feeling about him. He's good.

Kitty would roll her eyes and mutter, *A feeling, well that's great. I'm sure Ted Bundy's victims all had a feeling about him, too.*

No doubt Kitty would be right in urging caution. Maggie was so lonely and so desperate for kindness she probably was an easy mark at this point, but she *did* have a good feeling about Nick. He was handsome with his dark brown hair and dark brown eyes, and his heavy New York accent was charming, if a little difficult to understand. But that wasn't why Maggie felt safe with him. It wasn't the uniform, either. She had encountered other policemen, and none of them made her want to throw herself into their arms. There was really no good reason to trust him; she just did.

"Here we are," he said at last.

To Maggie it sounded like, "Hee we ah," and she smiled.

"Why are you smiling like that?" he asked. His tone was gentle, and so were his eyes as they probed her expression.

"Your accent. It's, um, cute." She blushed. She had no experience with men outside of Mathew, and she didn't want to give him the wrong idea or make him think she was hitting on him.

"Maybe you're the one with the accent; did you ever think of that, Miss Montana?"

"I know someone who almost was Miss Montana," she said. His remark made her think of Marcus Henshaw's girlfriend who had been a runner up for Miss Montana. She blushed again as she realized Nick probably wouldn't find that interesting. Back home in her small community it was big news.

"Is it you?" he asked. He winked at her before turning to lead his horse into the stable.

Her mouth opened slightly in surprise. Was he flirting with her? She shook her head. Of course not. They were strangers, and he was obviously older than her.

"How old are you?" she asked as she caught up with him.

"Twenty three."

"That's young to be a police officer."

"I graduated high school when I was seventeen. Got a two-year degree in criminal justice, went to the police academy, and here I am. What about you, how old are you?"

"Eighteen."

He whistled. "You're only a baby. How did someone so young find herself engaged?"

"In Montana it's not so unusual. We get married younger there." Eighteen was still young, even by Montana standards, but she didn't want him to think she was a stupid kid. "Besides, we were neighbors. We knew each other our whole lives and spent almost every day together."

He smiled, and it looked genuine. "Sounds like my mom and dad."

"Are your parents still together?" she asked.

"They would be, but my dad died when I was young."

"I'm very sorry. My mom died when I was six. It's…hard to be without a parent. What did your father die of?" She wondered if he would say he was a police officer who died in the World Trade Center. That was her only experience of New York.

"He was in the navy when he was young. Some of the stuff he worked with gave him lung cancer. What about your mom?"

"Breast cancer. Do you have siblings?"

"No, but I have cousins. Lots and lots of cousins." His tone was rueful. "What about you?"

"I have three older sisters."

"Are they as pretty as you?"

"Oh, no, they're much prettier."

He caught a glimpse of her out of the corner of his eye and realized he was making her uncomfortable. He needed to keep in mind she had recently lost her fiancé.

"I'm always like this, if it makes you feel any better," he said. "I'm sort of a flirt. Don't take it personally; I'm offering you a friendly shoulder, all right?"

Said any other way his comment might have embarrassed or hurt her, but he said it with such kindness and sincerity she could only smile. "All right. Thank you. I do appreciate it. I'm afraid I don't have much experience with men outside of my family and Mathew."

He nodded as if he understood, but he didn't. The girls of his acquaintance had too much experience, especially girls as pretty as Maggie. He had never met anyone as innocent as she appeared to be.

She helped him remove his saddle, curry, and feed his horse. It occurred to him she probably knew more about horses than he did, but the thought was more fascinating than galling. Her face was radiant as she talked softly to the horse. Without her grief she was even more beautiful.

She's supposed to be happy, he thought. A girl like her is supposed to be loved, protected, and provided for. Cherished.

The unbidden and foreign thoughts made him turn away from her and shake his head. What was wrong with him? He was a notorious free agent with no plans to settle down any time this decade. Why was a girl he had known for a half hour having this effect on him? He needed to say goodbye and walk away right now, but he had promised her dinner. *Later,* he told himself. *I'll say goodbye later.*

But as the evening wore on he was finding it more and more difficult to leave Maggie. He took her for pizza and laughed when she had no idea what he was talking about.

"A pie, you know," he said. "A slice."

"You eat pie for supper?" she asked.

"A pizza pie," he clarified.

"Oh, right, sorry. Do you come with some sort of translation manual?"

He grinned at her. "I can see we're going to have to start with the basics and work our way up from there."

When they reached the restaurant, he cleared away her utensils.

"Watch and learn," he said when the pizza arrived. He picked up one of the large slices, folded it in half and took a bite. The cheese burned the roof of his mouth and he winced.

"Watch and learn," she said. She took a piece of pizza, blew on it until it was cool, and then took a delicate bite.

"Showoff," he accused.

After supper he showed her some of the more popular tourist sights in Manhattan. The urge to take her hand was overpowering, but he resisted the impulse. He knew it would scare her off, and rightly so. They were strangers.

"Do you live around here?" she asked.

"No, I live in Bensonhurst. That's an old, Italian neighborhood in Brooklyn, worlds away from here." His eyes looked far off, and she guessed he was thinking of his home.

"Not as far as Montana," she said.

"I'm not sure about that," he said cryptically.

"Did you go to one of those schools with initials?" she asked.

It took him a moment to figure out what she meant. "Yes, I went to PS 128 for grammar school."

"I've never understood what the PS stands for," she said. "Is it some New York code?"

He pressed his lips together. "It means Public School."

Her mouth opened slightly in surprise at her own ignorance. "Oh. That's the sort of thing my sister, Kitty, would make fun of me for. Thank you for refraining."

"You're welcome, so long as you realize it's taking a lot of effort. What was the name of your school?"

"Kitchen," she said. At his puzzled look she continued. "I was homeschooled. After my mother died there was no one to make the hour-long drive to town."

"You really live that far away from town?" he asked.

"Yes. My dad owns a ranch that has been in our family for four generations. We own ten thousand acres, give or take."

He stopped dead. "Ten thousand acres?" He had a difficult time imagining such a massive spread of land.

"That's not much. Mathew's parents own double that amount, and then some."

It sounded as if her fiancé had been wealthy. He didn't want to dwell on why that thought disturbed him.

When he could think of no more reasons to keep her out, he took her home. It was late by the time they arrived. He didn't even want to think what time it would be when he finally arrived at his own home, over an hour and a half away by subway.

"Your aunt has some fancy digs," he commented. She lived in a large brownstone with a doorman.

"Really?" Maggie asked. She sounded truly shocked. "But it's so tiny. It only has two bedrooms and two bathrooms."

He pinched his leg to keep from laughing. "In Manhattan, that's the equivalent of your ranch."

"Oh." Her face puckered as she processed that. Previously she had felt sorry for her aunt and assumed she was poor. Now that she knew the truth it put a new light on things and made it more difficult to accept her constant criticism.

"What's that face for?" He already hated the utter curiosity about her that made him desperate to know what she was feeling and thinking.

"Nothing, I'm realizing how little I know about the world, and New York in particular."

"I could help you with that," he heard himself volunteer. What was wrong with him? Was he on some sort of self-destruct mission? He needed to get away from her, not think up new ways to see her.

"How so?"

"Think of me as your tour guide." *Or don't. Please save me from myself and walk away.* "I'll show you what you need to know to survive, and then I'll show you what you need to fall in love. With the city," he added hastily. Was he blushing? Oh, geez, he was.

If she recognized any aberration in his tone or speech she didn't let on. "Are you sure you don't mind?" She peered shyly up at him through her lashes. Some girls had tried that look on him, and he always saw through it as being calculated and practiced. With Maggie, it was an unconscious gesture born out of uncertainty and bashfulness.

"It's my duty." He tapped his chest and realized he wasn't wearing his badge, so in essence he had tapped his heart. *Oh, geez, I've got to get away before I make an even bigger fool of myself.* "No arguments," he told her. "Meet me at the same place, same time tomorrow."

"All right," she agreed softly. "Thank you so much, Nick." She smiled. He smiled.

When she turned to go inside, he realized he was still staring at the spot she had been, grinning like a complete idiot.

CHAPTER 10

For the next few weeks they went out every night and weekend. Nick's family was urging him to introduce them to his new girl.

"We're only friends," he reiterated for the eightieth time that week.

"Sure, Nicky," was the most common response.

If they could see him and Maggie together, they wouldn't have any doubts. They talked endlessly about the events of their days, family, movies, television, music, and even sports and horses. But they never touched. Not even a casual goodnight kiss or a clasping of hands.

For Nick it was a first. He had a well-earned reputation in his neighborhood for taking a girl out once and never seeing her again. He had left a trail of broken hearts all over Brooklyn, and never once felt bad about jilting a girl he was dating.

And then he met Maggie.

Now he was eating his heart out on a daily basis, and she had no idea. At first he tried to mask his feelings for her, but he soon realized she was oblivious, not only to him, but to the effect she had on everyone. She had no idea how pretty she was. She didn't see people stop and look at her, arrested by her large eyes and sweet smile. She didn't notice the way cabbies and street-hardened sales clerks bent over backwards to take care of her and be nice to her. As soon as Nick realized this he allowed himself to stare at her unabashedly whenever she wasn't looking, and he had no qualms about setting up daydreams with the two of them as the stars. He harbored a secret dream that if he put in enough time being her friend, she would magically wake up one day and realize she was in love with him, although he was beginning to have his doubts about his plan. For days at a time she would be normal, and then suddenly her eyes would be red and puffy, and he knew she was mourning her lost love.

He began to ask himself what Mathew Henshaw had that he didn't. And for the first time in his life he was jealous of another man. It was made worse by the fact that his competition wasn't alive to compete with. How could he hope to compare with a memory? And, according to Maggie, Mathew was perfect in every way: kind, courteous, attentive, thoughtful, strong, patient, kind, and funny. *I'm all those things,* he wanted to yell, but he knew it would do no good. It was too soon. She wasn't ready to move on, and the more he got to know her, he wondered if she would ever be ready. She was a deep soul. Once she became attached to someone there was no letting go, and she had eighteen years of time and memories with Mathew.

So Nick bided his time, day after day, patiently building a friendship with Maggie. He tried to content himself in the fact that she depended on him as she did no one else in the city, but he was haunted by the fact that at any moment she could disappear and go back to Montana, in which case she would be out of his grasp forever. And every day he became a little more heartsick, waiting and hoping Maggie would notice him.

Maggie did notice Nick, but not in the way he wanted. *He's such a good friend,* was her nearly constant thought. He was caring and fun. Most important of all, he was *there.* He made her feel safe. Every day, without fail, he was with her, showing her the sights of the city and teaching her to love them. When she was with him, she could forget everything else, at least for the length of time they were together. She forgot her grief, her homesickness, and her difficult relationship with her aunt. For the few hours they were together every day, she was a normal girl exploring the city with a handsome boy. Sometimes she stole surreptitious glances at him. If the situation were different, if there had never been a Mathew and she hadn't lost him in such a heinous manner, then maybe she and Nick would have dated. Whenever these thoughts occurred to her she banished them with haste. They were embarrassing, especially because he most likely didn't view her that way. After all, he was five years older and a real grown up with a real job in one of the largest and most interesting cities in the world. She was a girl from Montana who now had no idea what to do with her life.

Currently that issue was the biggest one creating strife in her living situation.

"Are you simply going to live off my largess forever?" her aunt asked on an almost daily basis.

Maggie didn't point out to her it wasn't completely the case. Her father had sent her with ten thousand dollars that she was using to pay a small rent to her aunt, and she ate out every night with Nick, so her food was covered, too. The few attempts she had made to defend herself fell on deaf ears, so she simply kept silent and waited for the moment she could leave the house with Nick.

"What's wrong?" Nick asked as soon as he met her in the park a couple of months after their first meeting.

Maggie shook her head.

"Fight with the aunt?" he guessed.

She expelled a sigh. "Yes, but it's not that big a deal, and she does have a point. I'm going to need to get a job eventually."

If she got a job she wouldn't be available as often. She might meet other people, people who could take advantage of her sweet, trusting nature. The more he got to know her, the more he learned his first impression of her was correct; if anyone needed a keeper it was Maggie Chapman.

"Take your time," he urged. "Don't rush into anything because your shrew of an aunt is pressuring you." He had only met the aunt once, but the meeting hadn't gone well. She was a west-side snob. At first sight of him her face had brightened with interest, and then she learned he was Bensonhurst born and bred, and her look changed to one of near-revulsion.

"Are you Italian or Jewish?" she had asked with only slightly masked disdain.

"Take your pick," he had said, "I've probably got a little of both in there somewhere." He was purely Italian, but many of his friends were Jewish, and her prejudiced attitude rankled him. After that, he met Maggie outside to avoid a second confrontation with her overbearing aunt. The thought of his sweet Maggie living with that witch day after day was painful to him.

"It's not so much what she says that bothers me," Maggie said. "It's that I had this dream it would be like having my mom back. My memories of her are fuzzy at best, and I thought living with my aunt might help me remember how it was." She paused. "Now I'm questioning the memories I do have. Was she like my aunt? Was she that mean, negative, and nasty all the time?"

Nick used her downcast mood as an opportunity to put his arm around her shoulders and give them a squeeze. "Just because they're sisters doesn't mean they were exactly alike. You're different from your sisters, aren't you?"

"Yes," she said. She brightened slightly.

"Besides," he kept his arm around her as they walked and talked. "Everything you've told me about your mom sounds wonderful. If you're a part of her, I know she was amazing."

She smiled up at him, and the elusive dimple in her cheek made an appearance. "Thanks, Nick. You're really good at making me feel better."

And really bad at making myself feel good, he thought. He reluctantly dropped his arm as the futility in the situation hit him anew.

"Hey, Marino," an aggravatingly familiar voice called.

He tried to keep walking but Maggie turned around with a smile. "Is that one of your friends?" she asked.

Nick blew out a breath. "No. He's a fellow cop. We were in the academy together. What's up, Edgerton?" He gave the approaching man an upward nod.

Todd Edgerton returned it, but he wasn't looking at Nick, he was looking at Maggie. With interest.

Nick placed his arm back around her shoulders.

"Who's your friend?" Edgerton asked.

When Nick didn't answer, Maggie held out her hand to the newcomer. "I'm Maggie."

"Maggie," Edgerton repeated. He bowed slightly and kissed the back of her hand. "Are you one of those models who only has one name?"

"No, I'm one of those sensible girls who doesn't give my last name to strangers," she said. It was a very "Kitty" thing to say, she thought, and smiled as she imagined her sister's approval.

"But I'm a cop," Edgerton said. "You can call me Edge. Everyone does."

He was giving her what was probably a flirtatious smile, but Maggie had no interest in him, despite the fact that he was very nice looking. His light blond hair and blue eyes were a reminder of Mathew, and she simply wanted to get away from him. She moved closer to Nick, glad for his strength.

Edgerton looked between them. "Oh, I see how it is."

Neither Maggie nor Nick bothered to correct his assumption.

"She's not your usual type, Marino, but I guess you've cycled through all the girls in Brooklyn by now." He flashed a grin, and Maggie fought the urge to wrinkle her nose. She was glad Nick wasn't friends with him so she didn't have to pretend to like him. "How's life in the security guard business?"

Nick's eyes narrowed and he tightened his grip slightly on Maggie's shoulders. "Work's fine, Edge. How about you?"

"Can't complain. Interrupted a holdup last week. Helped the DEA bring down a drug smuggler. Handled a murder and an attempted kidnapping." He grinned again. "The usual."

Now Maggie did wrinkle her nose at him. Since when was a murder cause for jubilation, she wanted to ask.

Edge noticed her expression, and his smile widened. "Looks like your lady has no taste for police work," he said. "I guess she chose the right guy. See you later, Marino. Give my best to your horse." He turned and went away, leaving Maggie and Nick frowning at his retreating backside.

"I don't like that man," Maggie said.

"Me, neither," Nick agreed.

"What was that crack about you being a security guard?" she asked. She didn't usually pick up on subtle nuances in conversation, but Edge's inference had been crystal clear.

A part of him didn't want to tell her, but he realized with glee he trusted her enough to do so. Nothing he told Maggie would change her opinion of him. "A lot of cops look down on those of us who work in Central Park. It's considered sort of a cake job, like glorified security guards."

She nodded. She sensed there was more he wasn't telling her. "Is there a reason you do it?" She had noticed that many of the other men in his precinct were significantly older than him, and now that made sense if it was considered a softer job.

"Let's sit," he said. He led her to the stairs of a nearby church. "I used to work the fifth precinct. That covers Chinatown, Little Italy, and the Brooklyn Bridge. That area's all right during the day, but at night when I worked, things could get crazy, and usually did. My best buddy from the neighborhood was assigned the same area. We weren't together, because we were both rookies. But one night there was a gang riot, and we both showed up with our partners." He paused. She sensed what was coming and took his hand. He clung tightly to it as if it were a lifeline. "He got shot. He didn't make it. After that I lost my heart for the job. I had been so gung-ho, thinking I could change the world. I was the one who convinced him to be a cop with me, you know?" He shook his head. "So I put in for a transfer to the park. It's been sort of healing being in nature and riding the horse every day."

Unbidden, she put her arms around him and pressed her head to his chest. His arms encircled her, and they hugged in silence for a few minutes.

"We have a lot in common for two people who live worlds apart," she said.

His heart beat faster. He had never considered that before, but they had both lost a parent and a best friend. Maybe he somehow sensed their commonality, and it in some way explained his deep and instant attraction to her.

Maggie was glad to be giving comfort instead of receiving for once. Nick had been her constant support and companion for the last two months, and she owed him this much. Plus she had to admit she liked hugging him. His arms were warm, strong and secure. She had always been physically affectionate, and she was starving for human contact. Maybe that was why her mouth suddenly went dry and her heart picked up its pace. The scent of his cologne drifted into her nose, and she clenched her arms slightly before coming to her senses. *This isn't Mathew.* She released Nick and jumped away like she had been branded.

"Are you hungry?" she asked to cover her awkward movement.

"All right," he said. He followed her to their favorite restaurant without a word, but his eyes were troubled as he tried to figure her out.

CHAPTER 11

Two weeks later Maggie got a job.

Nick's insistence she become familiar with the city was having its desired effect on her, and she started venturing out more on her own during the daytime while he worked. On one such occasion she stopped in a delicatessen that was looking for someone to work the cash register. She was hired on the spot and set to begin work a few days later.

Strangely, when she excitedly told Nick the news, he was subdued.

"Aren't you happy?" she asked. "I got a job. A real, grown up job."

Finally her enthusiasm caught and he smiled, too. "Yes, I'm very happy for you. You're going to be the best cashier ever." He picked her up in a spontaneous hug, and when he set her down there was a slight awkwardness between them. On his part it was because he wanted so much more than that one small hug.

"At least this should make my aunt happy," Maggie said.

But it didn't.

"A cashier?" she repeated when Maggie told her about it. "You can't make enough to live on if you had three of those jobs full time, and you're only going to be working part time. What kind of career is that?"

"It's not a career," Maggie defended. "It's a first job. I don't know how to do anything else, and I'm not sure what I want to do." She was hoping the new job would buy her some time so she could think about her future. Now that the shroud of grief was lifting she was starting to feel a slight panic about her life. What *was* she going to do? Even if she returned to Montana, she couldn't simply continue living off her father's dime indefinitely. But every time she tried to think of a plan she came up blank.

Her aunt continued on her rant as if Maggie hadn't spoken. "I told my sister not to marry that backwoods hillbilly. But, no, she had to do things her way. She ran off to the middle of nowhere, had a litter of children, and now she's dead. At least maybe I can have some sway with you so you don't end up the same way."

Maggie's eyes rounded and filled with tears, but her aunt wasn't looking at her so she had no idea how hurtful her words were. Or maybe she did and simply didn't care because she kept speaking.

"If she had married that senator's son and stayed in civilization like normal people, none of this would have happened, and she would still be alive," she said.

"Y-you think marrying my dad and having my sisters and I is what killed my mother?" Maggie asked.

"No," Victoria said with forced patience. "Living far from medical care killed her. Didn't anyone ever tell you they didn't find her cancer until it was too far gone? I'm sure your father was too busy using her as a breeder for his children to allow her any sort of medical care. And then once the cancer was finally found, she had to drive all that way to seek treatment." She shook her head. "If she had been somewhere closer to medical care, she would have lived; I'm sure of it."

Maggie felt like the rug had been pulled out from under her world. She didn't know what had transpired with her mother's illness. All she knew was that her mother had fought a losing battle with cancer for most of Maggie's first six years. She didn't remember her when she wasn't sick. But her aunt's words had the sting of truth in them. They did live far from any sort of medical facility. Every time her mother had a treatment the family had to go to Billings, two hours away by car and train. And her father hated doctors. He avoided them if at all possible, even once having their cowboy Rook sew up his hand when he cut it to the bone. Had he disallowed his wife from going to the doctor until it was too late to save her? If her mother had lived somewhere else or married someone else, would she still be alive? Had she, Maggie, not only caused Mathew's death, but in a roundabout way participated in her mother's demise as well?

Her aunt raged on, but Maggie tuned her out. She couldn't take any more. Inside she was hollow. This new pain went too deep for words or tears. Finally, blessedly, her aunt went out for the evening. Maggie lay listlessly on the couch, so far gone she forgot to go downstairs to meet Nick.

Nick waited for only a few minutes before going upstairs to seek Maggie. She was at times scatterbrained, but he knew she looked forward to their outings together, and she had never been late. For her to be late now was alarming.

There was no answer at the door, and when he tried the handle it was unlocked. His heart thudded painfully in his chest, and he wished for his gun. Doors were never, ever, ever left unlocked in New York, and if they were it was usually a sign something bad had already happened.

But when he opened the door, he saw Maggie lying on the couch, staring pitifully into space. She blinked at him, but otherwise didn't indicate she noticed his presence.

His relief at seeing her intact was palpable but short-lived. Obviously something was terribly wrong with her. He knelt in front of her and smoothed his hand over her forehead a couple of times. In all their time together he tried to refrain from touching her and scaring her off, but seeing her in such pain forced him to reach out.

"What happened?" he asked.

His gentle tone was her undoing. She burst into tears and pressed her face to his shoulder. He moved closer and gathered her to him. She sobbed for a long while, and when she was finished, she still couldn't tell him. Somehow she was shamed by her aunt's accusation, and she couldn't share it with Nick. She didn't want anyone to know she might have been a factor in her mother's death, or that her beloved father might have contributed by denying care. Instead she shook her head against his shoulder.

Inside, Nick's heart was breaking. Seeing Maggie this upset and in this much pain was akin to a physical injury. He couldn't take it. He had to fix it, no matter what. She didn't realize it yet, but she was his, and he would do whatever was necessary to protect her.

"Was it your aunt?" he tried, and failed, to keep the harshness out of his tone. He hated her aunt the way he hated criminals on the street. To him there was no difference between them; they both preyed on the weak and innocent.

She nodded.

He took a deep breath and tried to think. What he was about to do was major, but there was no other way. He couldn't leave her any longer with a woman so bent on breaking her gentle spirit. If today was any indication, then the odious Victoria was close to succeeding. He pulled away slightly and framed her face with his hands.

"Maggie, you're not staying here any longer. I want you to pack your bags. You're coming home with me."

Her mouth fell open and she gasped. "I can't live with you. My dad would kill me."

He smiled. "Did I forget to tell you I live with my Mom? Your virtue is safe." Safe from his actions, if not his intentions, anyway. His mother would make sure of it.

"Nick, I appreciate that, but I'm already a burden here. At least my aunt is family. I can't burden you and your mother this way."

"You're not a burden," he assured her. "You're my friend, and you need help. Maybe without your aunt's constant attacks and criticism you'll be able to think clearly enough to figure out what you want to do."

"But my job," she protested. She had been looking forward to working for the first time ever.

"There are plenty of jobs in my neighborhood. People know me and my mom there. You won't have any trouble getting one. Only, how is your Italian?" He winked at her to let her know he was teasing.

Mostly. Their neighborhood was filled with Italian specialty shops, and many of the people did speak English as a second language, despite the fact that they were third or fourth generation Americans.

She giggled and the sound made him smile. She hugged his neck tightly. "Nick, you're too good to me. What would I do without you?"

I don't intend to ever let you find out, he thought, and he was startled by the permanence of his resolution. For the first time he realized how deep his feelings for her went. Maggie wasn't a crush or a passing fancy. He was in love with her, and he wanted her for the rest of his life. *But how to convince her we belong together,* he wondered, and then he helped her pack.

CHAPTER 12

Maggie was nervous, and so was Nick. They sat in the taxi anxiously clasping hands on the long ride to Bensonhurst. It was going to cost a fortune, but she had too many bags to take on the subway. Plus this way she would see the nicer parts of his neighborhood and not the seedy underbelly near the subway station. She stared out the window, lost in thought and introspection, and he stared at her.

He was somewhat nervous about the neighborhood's reaction to her. It was no secret he had been with her every single day for almost three months, and people were falling all over themselves with curiosity about his mystery girl. She would no doubt be the subject of much gossip and speculation for the next few days or weeks. That was to be expected.

What bothered him the most was his mother's possible reaction to her. Like a good Italian mother she was overprotective of her only son. She had practically loathed every girl he ever dated, and they had all been Italian, Catholic, and from the neighborhood. Now he was bringing her an Anglo-Saxon protestant from Montana. Not only that, but he was bringing her to live with them in their tiny apartment. He shifted uncomfortably. His mother wasn't soft with her opinions. If she didn't approve, she would make no secret of the fact, and she could make Maggie's life as unpleasant as her aunt had.

The closer they got to his home, the more his doubts increased. What had seemed like a good idea at the time might turn out to be a disaster, and not only from his perspective. If Manhattan scared Maggie, how would she react to Brooklyn? He began to look at his neighborhood through her eyes. He saw the trash piling up on the sidewalks, waiting for the garbage men and causing a stink. There were shops with signs in every language. There were no high rises, only small and medium-sized buildings.

When they arrived Maggie turned to him. "This is your building?"

He nodded. If she had thought her aunt's luxurious Manhattan apartment was poor living, what must she think of their lackluster apartment?

"I love it," she said enthusiastically. "All of it. This neighborhood, this building, it feels much homier than Manhattan. Everything there is so glossy. You get the feeling no one lives in all those pretty buildings. But here is where people really live." She pointed to a patio decked with every conceivable flower and herb. "Beautiful."

"That's Mrs. Esposito. Don't get her talking about her plants. You'll never get away." He grinned at her. He was delighted she liked his home. She returned his smile, and for a moment they were caught up in looking at each other until the cabbie spoke.

"Yous getting out, or what?"

"Keep your shirt on," Nick snapped.

A few months ago the exchange might have disturbed Maggie, but now she realized it was simply how people talked to each other here. It was a different place, but she was learning to love it.

Nick felt every eye in the neighborhood on them as he and Maggie unloaded her bags from the trunk of the cab. He wondered how long it would take for the curiosity seekers to start pestering him. Not long, as it turned out.

"Hey, Nicky, is that your new girl?" Mrs. Gallo stuck her head out of her third floor window and hollered. "She's movin' in, eh? Your mamma didn't mention that."

"Hi, Mrs. Gallo," he called politely, and then ushered Maggie inside with expediency. He knew his mother would learn of his arrival before they made it into the apartment, and, sure enough, when he opened the door she was facing them, her dark eyes snapping fire.

"Ma," he said slowly, warningly, "this is Maggie Chapman."

His mother's eyes turned from him to Maggie who had dropped her bag and was now nervously clasping her hands in front of her. Her big eyes were hopeful and apprehensive. She bit her lip, and then let it go to smile at his mother. "Hello, Mrs. Marino," she said softly. "You have a lovely home, and son." She gave a tentative smile.

Nick knew that was the exact instant his mother fell in love with Maggie. She smiled and went forward to hug the younger girl. "I'm so happy to finally meet you, Maggie. My son hasn't told me nearly enough about you it seems." She pinched Nick's arm. Hard.

He winced and drew away from her. "Ouch, Ma." He rubbed his sore arm. "Maggie's had a bad turn with her aunt. I was hoping she could stay with us a little while."

"You can stay as long as you like, dear," she said to Maggie. She still hadn't released her from her hug, and now Maggie melted into her embrace.

Maggie thought she had never encountered anything as comforting as Nick's mother's embrace. It was different to be hugged by a mother, she realized. She had hugged lots of people in her life, but none offered her the care and comfort of this woman. Despite the fact they were almost equal in size this woman had a strength unlike anything Maggie had ever encountered. She knew in the instant they touched that Mrs. Marino would most likely kill someone with her bare hands if it meant protecting her son, and now she was extending that same protection to her. For Maggie, who had always craved a mother and had recently left her cold, distant aunt, the moment went to her very soul. Tears filled her eyes and she quickly dashed them away before they could overflow.

"Thank you," she said, although the words were difficult to get out because her throat was choked with emotion. "Nick has been wonderful to me, and he's helped me more than you can imagine. I see where he gets his kindness." Maggie reluctantly withdrew and then smiled at Mrs. Marino.

Mrs. Marino let her go. "Call me Edda," she said. "And I see Nico hasn't told you his name, either."

"Ma," Nick said. The Americanization of his given name had been an argument between them since he started grammar school.

"Nico," Maggie repeated. "I like that." She stole a glance at Nick.

He raised an eyebrow at her. "Do you want me to call you Margaret?"

"No one else does."

He thought that over. "Maybe I will sometimes."

They shared a smile.

Edda looked between them and beamed. She would never admit it to Nick, but she liked the improvements she saw in him lately. His previous playboy lifestyle had left a lot to be desired. The endless line of girls he paraded before her left a lot to be desired, too. Edda had a keen sense about people and what she read in their eyes didn't spell marriage and commitment.

Maggie Chapman, though, was a whole different creature. True, she wasn't Catholic, but there were worse things. In the almost three months her son had been taking her out, he had settled down into the respectable young man she had raised him to be. He was making her proud, and his soft heart for Maggie was further proof of that. And it didn't take a second look at the girl to know she was everything a mother desired for her son: wholesome, sweet, and good. The type of girl that would provide grandbabies and then be an excellent mother to them.

She put an arm around Maggie and led her to the couch. "Tell me about yourself, Maggie. Nico, take her bags to your room. We'll keep them in there."

Maggie sat and brushed a stray hair out of her eyes. Were all people in New York as kind and welcoming as Nick and Edda, she wondered. And then she thought of her aunt and realized the answer was no.

"My family owns a ranch in Montana. That's where I grew up," she began.

"What brought you to New York?" Edda asked. Nick had only told her Maggie was from out of town and needed his help becoming familiar with the city. At the time she had worried the stranger had designs on her stable, policeman son. Now the thought was laughable. Maggie wore every expression on her face, and she had no hidden agenda. She was like a sweet little lamb, and Edda was suddenly glad her son had been there to protect her all these months. Who knew what might have happened to her without Nico to watch over her?

Maggie touched the third finger of her left hand, drawing Edda's gaze there. What she saw froze her heart. She was wearing an engagement ring. Surely Nico wouldn't take such a big step without telling her first, would he?

"My fiancé was killed by a man who was trying to abduct me. I had to leave home to get away, and I haven't been able to contact my family since." Her lips quivered and her eyes filled with tears.

"Oh, my poor dear," Edda said. Once again she pulled Maggie into a hug, and once again Maggie experienced comfort on a level she had never imagined.

This is what I've been missing without a mother, she thought. Her sister Libby had been a good substitute, but she was only four years older, after all.

"You're safe now," Edda promised her. "Nico and I will take care of you in any way we can."

Nick entered the room and looked at the picture his mother and Maggie made together. Something turned over in his heart. His mother had never approved of his girlfriends, and, until now, he hadn't realized how much was missing in his life without that approval. His mother looked at him over Maggie's shoulder and smiled. He returned her smile, and something passed between them.

They would take care of her as if she were their own, and if either of them had any say in the matter, someday she would belong to them completely.

CHAPTER 13

aggie felt torn. She knew she was welcome at the Marino's apartment. Besides the fact that they told her as much on a daily basis, they made it clear in the loving way they extended hospitality to her. Neither Nick nor his mother would hear of taking money from her, even though she still had plenty from what her father had given her.

But despite their warm and welcoming attitude, she knew she was in the way. She had never felt like more of an obstruction or burden in her life. In some ways it was worse than living with her aunt. Her aunt had made it clear she was an interloper. The Marinos smiled cheerfully at her, despite the fact that she was very obviously disrupting their routine and crowding their living space.

Like her aunt, the Marinos had two bedrooms. Unlike her aunt, they only had one bathroom. Their apartment was also smaller over-all. The two bedrooms were small, and then there was one room that contained the kitchen and living room. Maggie slept on the couch and tried hard to stay out of their way in the mornings when they were getting ready for work. During the day she tried to make herself useful by cleaning the apartment, but it only took a short time to clean the small space. She would have volunteered to cook, but she didn't know how. And she definitely didn't know how to cook the authentic Italian food they ate every night. Her sister, Libby, was an excellent cook, but Maggie secretly thought she had nothing on Edda Marino.

The older woman made incredible concoctions. Most nights Maggie couldn't pronounce them, but they were always delicious, and almost all of them contained homemade pasta and homemade sauce. Edda even went so far as to make her own mozzarella and ricotta cheeses.

When she couldn't serve a purpose in the apartment, she edged her way outside and met some of the neighbors. She started first with Mrs. Esposito, the woman who owned the balcony garden. The old woman met her knock with suspicion, but that quickly changed to delight when Maggie asked to see her garden.

"You like gardening?" the woman asked. Her accent was a mixture of New York and Italian. Maggie had to lean in close to catch what she said.

"I do," Maggie answered. She went on to tell her about her garden in Montana.

Mrs. Esposito had trouble conceiving of a home garden that covered half an acre.

"My sister does a lot of canning," Maggie told her. "And cowboys eat a lot."

The old woman nodded approvingly. "I would like to meet this sister. She sounds like the right sort of girl."

"That would be lovely," Maggie agreed. "But she's expecting a baby soon, and is unable to travel." Her smile fled. How did Libby look pregnant, she wondered. Was her husband Dobbie fussing over her like a mother hen? She fought back tears.

Mrs. Esposito took her hand. "Come to my balcony. It will cheer you up."

And it did. Maggie had always found healing in nature, even if it was a five foot section of flowers and herbs. She surprised Mrs. Esposito by naming all the different plant varieties.

"I like you," Mrs. Esposito declared. "You're going to be good for Nicky."

Maggie blushed and pressed her lips together. "He's a good friend."

"Hmph," Mrs. Esposito said. "Kids today and their 'friends.' In my day we didn't have friends. You dated a boy or you didn't. Life was simpler then."

"I imagine it was," Maggie agreed. Her tone was wistful. She had often thought she was born out of time. She should have been raised in the nineteen fifties when nothing more was expected of her than to marry well and raise children.

In addition to Mrs. Esposito, she met the DeLucas. The young husband and wife were both attorneys, born and raised in Manhattan.

"Why did you move to Bensonhurst?" Maggie asked curiously. As far as she could tell everyone was trying to work his or her way up to Manhattan.

"We've always loved Brooklyn," Mrs. DeLuca answered. "Bensonhurst is dying out. The old neighborhoods are fading away. We're both Italian, and we wanted to do something to pass along our heritage to our children."

They had two small children who adored Maggie on sight. The feeling was mutual for her. Whenever she wasn't visiting with Mrs. Esposito, she was playing with the DeLuca children. They were both in preschool, but she saw them every afternoon when they arrived home.

She loved the Marinos. She loved their neighbors. She even loved Brooklyn, but she hated feeling like a burden. After a week and a half of feeling useless and in the way, Maggie confronted Nick. Edda left to meet with a group from their church, and they had the apartment to themselves.

"Nick, I really appreciate you and your mom taking me in like this."

"It's no bother," Nick said. He sensed a "but" coming, and he was right.

"But I can't stay here," she added.

They had been slouched together on the couch watching television. Now he sat up straight and muted the television. "What are you talking about?" Was she going back to Montana already?

"I'm in the way here. I hate feeling like a burden."

"You're not a burden," he argued. "We love having you here."

She smiled and pressed her palm to his cheek. He couldn't stop himself from closing his eyes and leaning into her touch. "You're very sweet, and so is your mother, but you don't have to take care of me. I'm not your responsibility."

He opened his eyes. She was right; he had no claim to her. The thought made his heart sink. He *wanted* to be responsible for her. He wanted to take care of her. He was amazed at the way she fit seamlessly into his life. His mother loved her. His cousins loved her, at least the few of them she had met. Even his taciturn neighbor, Mrs. Esposito, had smacked him over the head with her paper and told him to "wise up and stake a claim on the girl before she gets away."

"I could get an apartment of my own nearby," Maggie was saying. "I still have money from my dad. It would be enough for a couple of months rent while I find a job."

The thought of her living alone, even in this relatively safe neighborhood, sent a shudder through him.

"You can't live alone here, Maggie."

"But," she started, but he interrupted her.

"Did you forget you're being hunted?" Maybe it was unfair to bring up her stalker, but it was a truth that needed to be dealt with.

She winced. "No, but he doesn't know where I am."

"I've studied stalkers. He won't stop until somebody stops him. I'm not taking that chance with your safety."

"But Nick, I can't live on your couch forever. Even if you and your mother are too polite to say it, I'm in the way, and I know it. You don't have to take care of me."

"Someone has to," he said bluntly. He took her hands in his. "Maggie, I don't want to hurt your feelings or wound your pride, but you're not equipped to handle this city on your own. You need someone to take care of you."

It was painful to hear. Perhaps more so because she knew it was true. Before him she had Kitty and Mathew to oversee her care, to explain things to her and order her life for her. Now she was lost and alone. Without Nick she would be floundering, and she knew it.

"It shouldn't have to be you," she said. She withdrew her hands from his grasp and twisted them miserably in her lap. She hated herself at this moment. Why was everyone around her able to cope with life when she couldn't? How did everyone else grow to be a mature adult while she remained a little girl, hidden and sheltered from the world?

"I want it to be me," he said. He stilled her hands and took them again. "I have a solution that would get you off the couch and make you feel like a part of the family."

"What?" She looked at him with hope in her eyes.

"You could become a part of the family. You could marry me."

CHAPTER 14

"Marry you?" Maggie asked as if she couldn't believe the question, which she couldn't.

"Yes," Nick said. He sounded calm, but inside his heart was pounding. He felt as if his very life depended on her answer.

"I can't marry you," she said.

"Why not?"

"I'm not Catholic."

He chuckled. "If that's your biggest worry in the situation, then we're safe. My mother's father was protestant. We're not strangers to interfaith marriages."

"We barely know each other."

"We've spent every day of the last three months together. You know my mother and some of my craziest cousins. You know where I live, where I work, you even know my horse's name and his favorite snack." He squeezed her hand. "Besides all that we've talked about everything. You're the closest friend I have right now. If there's one person who knows me better than you, it's my mom."

It was true that they had spent every day of the last few months together, and they had talked about every subject under the sun. Some of the things she had shared with him she had only shared with Mathew, and that was after years of friendship and dating.

"We're not in love," she said.

Speak for yourself, he thought. Out loud he said, "We're good friends, and that's a great foundation. Despite our difference in geography we have things in common. Our temperaments match. My grandparents had an arranged marriage, and they had far less than we have together. They ended up falling in love and were very happy."

She looked up at him and her eyes penetrated to his soul. "Why would you do this?"

He opened his mouth to answer and found he couldn't. He might be able to offer himself in marriage, but he couldn't tell her how much he loved her when her heart still belonged to Mathew. "I care about you, about your wellbeing. I want to protect you. If we're married and something happens to me, I'll have the peace of mind you'll be taken care of by my survivor benefits."

Her eyes filled with tears and she gripped his hand. She didn't want to think about survivor benefits, and she especially didn't want to think about anything happening to Nick.

"Don't let anything happen to you," she said.

Her fervent tone gave him the hope he needed. She might not realize it because she was still healing, but she cared for him.

"I don't have plans to leave you any time soon."

They sat in oppressive silence while Maggie tried to think. She wasn't good at reasoning things out. Times like these were when Kitty stepped in to help her. She wasn't overbearing to the point of making decisions for her, she simply listed the pros and cons to help Maggie think more clearly. She tried to do that for herself now, but it was difficult with Nick watching her.

On the plus side, she liked him very much. In fact, she couldn't think of many people she liked more. He was kind, funny, and smart. She liked his family and his neighborhood. He was right, too. She did need someone to watch out for her. She was alone and not equipped to be that way. Her family had put her in the care of her aunt, not realizing that was akin to throwing her naked into barbed wire.

She tried to list the negatives, but couldn't think of any. Surely there were some, but her mind kept coming back to one word: alone. Without him, she was utterly and completely alone and at the mercy of a world she didn't understand and was ill-prepared to face. She wasn't aware of how sheltered her upbringing was until she faced a different lifestyle. Homeschooling in the wilderness of Montana had only exposed her to her family and neighbors. Beyond them she had no experience with the outside world, and if her aunt was any indication, she didn't want to know more.

"All right, Nick," she said at last. "I'll marry you; if you're sure it's what you want to do."

"I'm sure," he said. He sounded sure.

"And if your mother approves."

"She'll approve," he said with the same certainty.

"I do have one condition," she said.

"Name it." At this point he would concede to anything to seal the deal.

"I want to pay for the wedding with the money my father gave me." He started to protest but she held up a hand. "If he were here, he would insist on paying for it. Using his money will be like he's beside me and giving me away." Her voice broke.

He was feeling remorse for practically railroading her into the marriage. "We could ask him to come and give you away. We could ask his blessing."

She smiled, touched by his thoughtfulness. "No, we can't do that. I can't take any chance of endangering my family by contacting them. Maybe one of your uncles or cousins can give me away."

He smiled. "My uncle Vito and I have always been close."

"Uncle Vito it is, then." She smiled.

He wanted to kiss her, to hold her and tell her how happy he was about her answer, but he didn't want to scare her off so soon after she conceded to the wedding. Instead he sat back and unmuted the television.

Maggie sat back, too, a little shell-shocked. Once the shock wore off the sadness set in. She remembered Mathew's proposal in their fort almost four months ago. It had been the best and worst day of her life. She thought of the dozens of roses he had showered on her. Absently she touched his ring and realized she would have to remove it now. She wasn't ready, not by a long shot.

Tears clouded her vision but she escaped to the bathroom before they could spill over. She pressed a towel to her face, sobbed into it, and turned on the faucet to cover the sound. When at last her emotions were spent she turned off the faucet, dried her eyes, took her ring off her finger, and tucked it into the pocket of her pants.

By the time Edda returned from her meeting they were once again sitting sedately on the couch. Nick sat up and turned off the television.

"Ma, we have something to tell you. We're getting married."

She looked between them with mixed emotions. On the one hand she was hoping the two of them would get together. On the other hand they looked anything but together. She had walked in on one too many makeout sessions between her son and his various girlfriends to find his current behavior normal. He pled with his eyes for her not to comment, so she took a cue from them and remained nonchalant.

"That sounds very nice," she said calmly. "When is the date?"

Maggie and Nick looked at each other and Edda tried not to roll her eyes. They hadn't discussed a date. What *had* they talked about? Nothing, as it turned out. She sat in front of them and together they hashed out plans for a wedding.

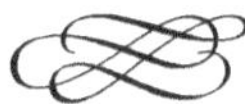

CHAPTER 15

They planned the wedding for the following Saturday. At first when Nick and Edda told her it would be a simple ceremony of immediate family, Maggie protested. She thought they were trying to keep costs down for her sake, and she told them to invite the neighborhood as well as their entire family.

Edda and Nick laughed for a long time.

"You don't know much about Catholics, do you?" Nick asked affectionately. "Mom has seven brothers, and there were ten children in my dad's family. Many of them have five to eight kids, and some of them have a handful of children, too. Inviting our immediate family would be well over a hundred people."

"Why are there so many?" she asked.

Nick flushed and looked away.

"Well, honey, traditionally Catholics don't believe in birth control," Edda said.

"Oh," Maggie said. Her mouth stayed puckered on the word.

"But I'm more progressive on my views in that area," Edda rushed to add. "You'll notice I only had one baby."

Later she arranged to get Nick out of the house so she could talk to Maggie alone. "Honey, Nico believes the same as I do concerning children. If you want to use birth control you'll have that option. With your unusual situation and young age it might best for awhile."

"Oh," Maggie said. Her mind was blank. She and Mathew hadn't planned on using birth control. They were hoping for children right away. Nick was a stranger, for all intents and purposes. She wasn't ready to bear his child. Her face flushed and her heart increased its rhythm. She was about to become his wife, with all the title implied. There was a good likelihood she might become pregnant. She wasn't ready to have someone else's baby. She wanted Mathew's baby.

"I think I might like to use birth control if you're sure it's all right with Nick," Maggie squeaked.

Edda nodded. This wasn't the conversation a bride should be having with her mother-in-law, but someone had to step in and help Maggie understand the reality of the situation before she found herself with a baby she wasn't ready for.

"My doctor is a very nice man. I'll make an appointment with him if you want."

Maggie nodded. She looked lost, alone, and afraid.

"And I'll go with you," Edda volunteered.

Some of Maggie's fear fled. She clasped the older woman's hand. "You would do that for me?"

"Of course I would." She patted Maggie's hand. Certainly she wasn't as innocent in this area as she appeared, was she? Edda knew few girls today saved themselves for marriage. Even in her day the notion had been scarce. Maggie had a serious boyfriend she was engaged to. Was it possible she was as naïve as she seemed?

She couldn't in good conscience allow her son to go through with the wedding without at least a word of warning.

"Nico, are you sure you know what you're getting yourself into with this marriage? The priest might allow you to marry a non-Catholic, but he won't permit a divorce."

"There won't be a divorce, Ma."

"She's young and innocent," she said, stolidly refusing to be dissuaded by his defensive tone.

"I know."

"And she's not over her other young man."

"I know," he said. His defensiveness fled and he sounded sad.

"Nico, are you sure you want to go through with this? You could court her and wait until she's ready."

He shook his head. "I feel like if we don't do this now I'm going to lose her. She's going to go back to Montana, or she's going to fall in with someone who will hurt her or take advantage of her. This is the best way I know of to protect her."

"What about when this business is over and she *can* go back to Montana? What then?"

Nick looked away, refusing to think about it. "Something will work out."

Edda opened her mouth and closed it again. She wasn't gaining any ground with him. He was obviously set on this marriage, and to keep pursuing all the difficulties facing the young couple might alienate them when they needed support the most.

"All right," she said at last. "But I'm here if you need anything, honey. Advice, or whatever."

"I know, Ma. Thanks." He smiled, and he looked optimistic once again.

Edda smiled, too, remembering when she had been young and in love and sure her life would work out fine. She hoped for their sakes it would.

The wedding went off without a hitch. Maggie met and liked Uncle Vito and was glad he was giving her away. She wasn't sure she would have been able to walk the aisle alone. The priest did a good job of performing the interfaith wedding. He had coached Maggie beforehand on the Catholic parts so she would know what to do. Nick beamed at her as she walked the aisle, and part of her wondered why. They were friends. He was doing this for her. Why did he look so happy about it?

She wanted to feel as happy as he looked, but instead she felt numb. If she allowed herself to feel anything it would be sadness this wasn't the wedding of her dreams and her groom wasn't Mathew, so instead she shut down her emotions and allowed her rational thoughts to guide her through the day. The ceremony was long and confusing, despite the priest's coaching. She was never sure when she was supposed to kneel. She was glad he was a kindly man who understood her confusion and prompted her on what to do.

She heard herself repeat the vows, but it felt like someone else was saying them. She hovered somewhere far away and detached, the same as she had when Mathew died. She saw and understood the events, but she couldn't believe she was participating in them. And then it was time for the kiss.

Maggie had never kissed anyone besides Mathew. Her heart fluttered, but there was no time to be nervous before Nick leaned down to place a soft kiss on her lips. But that's when everything went haywire because the touch of his lips on hers wasn't anything like the innocent touch she was used to. For a moment she thought he had shocked her, so acute was the sensation. It was over too quickly for her to figure out what had happened. He pulled away, and she was left blinking up at him in surprise.

He looked surprised, too, but pleasantly so. He gave her a half smile that set her heart beating twice its normal speed. Belatedly she realized they were now supposed to walk back down the aisle, and she was still staring at him in silent wonder. The small audience laughed. Nick took her hand and propelled her beside him as they exited the church.

CHAPTER 16

The reception was much more comfortable. An aunt who lived in a large house on Long Island offered to host the entire family for a potluck. At first Maggie tried to keep up and learn names, but she was quickly overwhelmed and gave up. There were lots of Tonys and Marias, and that was as much as she remembered. She and Nick were separated as soon as they arrived, but she didn't mind; she liked his family very much. They were boisterous and sometimes overwhelmed her shy nature, but they were warm, welcoming, and funny, too.

The food was delicious. Nick briefly appeared by her side when it was time to eat. He rested his hand on the small of her back and leaned close to whisper in her ear.

"Don't let them try to make you say whose marinara is best."

The simple touch was possibly the most intimate one they had shared. She caught a whiff of his cologne, and her heart started to tap out a strange rhythm.

"Huh?" she asked dumbly.

"You'll see." He winked at her and disappeared again.

She didn't have long to stare at his retreating backside.

"Which manicotti do you prefer?" One of his aunts was standing beside her asking the question. Maggie thought she was one of the Marias, but she didn't risk using her name.

"They're all delicious," she said. She stared at the groaning food table trying to figure out what manicotti was.

"Yes, but there are four manicottis here today," the aunt persisted. "Which one appeals to you most?"

"Um," Maggie said. Her eyes darted around for a rescue. She didn't want to offend her new aunt, but she had no idea what she was talking about.

"Ma, leave her alone. You're scaring her." A girl who looked to be about Nick's age came, took Maggie by the hand, and led her away. "I'm Alessa," she said.

Maggie breathed a sigh of relief. "You were at the wedding." There were only a handful of people at the ceremony, and Maggie knew Alessa and Nick must be close for her to have made the cut.

Alessa nodded. "Nico and I are only a few days apart. For most of my life we lived in the same building, but now I live in Queens."

"What do you do there?" Maggie asked.

"I live there. I work in Manhattan. I'm a paralegal for a fancy-schmancy law firm. What do you do? I'm afraid I don't know much about you. To be honest the wedding came as a surprise to most of the family."

Maggie smiled. "It came as a surprise to us, too. I don't have a job right now. I'm looking, I suppose." She must sound like an idiot to this mature woman who had a steady career.

Alessa studied her new cousin. There was something sweet and trusting about her that engendered a protective feeling. Was that why Nick married her? It would certainly explain his bizarre behavior. The girl was undoubtedly pretty, but so were all the girls he dated. Her blondish hair and fair complexion were a stark contrast to the all the dark-haired relatives in the room. Alessa couldn't count the number of times Nick told her he had no plans to marry before his thirtieth birthday. She wondered if Maggie had any idea she had reformed such a die-hard bachelor. For the rest of the day she stuck by the young girl's side. She was too innocent to get dragged into their family's raging marinara war, which she undoubtedly would if Alessa let her go. As it was she had to fend off three aunts who came at her with spoons full of something to taste.

"How did you and Nico meet?" Alessa asked.

"At the park."

Alessa grimaced. "The park," she repeated ruefully.

"You don't like the park?" Maggie asked. She thought Central Park was beautiful. It was difficult to imagine anyone who felt differently.

"The park is fine. Nico working there is the problem. How do you feel about it?"

Maggie knew by the way Alessa was looking at her that she was supposed to have some insightful, well thought out answer.

"I want Nick to do what makes him happy. I trust he knows what's best." There. That sounded good. She meant it, for the most part; but if she were being truthful, she would admit she hadn't given the issue much thought. She had enjoyed meeting Nick every day in the park and spending time with the horses, but was that what he enjoyed? Was he happy at his job? "What do you think?" she asked Alessa.

"I think it's a waste of talent," Alessa said. "I know Aunt Edda is probably happy he's doing something less dangerous, but Nico hasn't been the same since he left the fifth precinct. He was a good cop. One in a million, I think. He kept a cool head in any situation, and he had a compassionate nature that made victims trust him. I've never seen him happier or more alive than he was then. He felt good about himself, about what he was doing. Lately it's like he's a shell of who he used to be."

"A shell?" Maggie echoed. To her Nick seemed larger than life. He was the hero who rescued her on an almost daily basis. He had served in that capacity since she met him three and a half months ago. If he was only a shell of his former self, then who was he really?

Alessa nodded. "Don't get me wrong; some of his impulsive nature needed to be tamed. He was always a daredevil and a risk taker. I'm glad that part of him is gone, but he was also more vibrant, more alive. Since he started working at the park he's subdued, like an old man. It's almost like," she paused, looked around, and then lowered her voice. "It's almost like he's afraid."

Maggie didn't think Nick was afraid of anything, but then again she didn't really know him. "Do you think he would be happier back at his old job?"

"I don't know. But I don't think he's happy where he's at. I think he's sort of stuck in between and waiting for the next big thing." She gave Maggie a surreptitious look. "Maybe you can help him figure out what that is."

Maggie didn't say so, but she doubted it. She couldn't figure out her own life, let alone help Nick figure out his.

"Did you know he won a medal?" Alessa asked. She was still whispering, so Maggie thought maybe Nick didn't want the information shared.

"For what?"

"For his actions on the day of the event when Dominic was killed. Rookies don't usually earn such distinction, but Nico was almost ashamed of it."

Maggie could understand that. The sheriff had told her she did a good job on the morning of Mathew's death. He told her she did everything right, everything she could have to save him. But his words left Maggie feeling hollow and bitter. What did it matter that she did everything correctly if Mathew still died?

Her eyes sought Nick across the room; they really did have a lot in common. No one would ever guess by looking at him he had lost his best friend in such a tragic manner. Maybe, as Alessa suggested, she could help him find his way again. And maybe, just maybe, he would help her find hers.

He felt her staring and turned to give her a smile and a wave.

"Eh, what are we doing keeping these two from their wedding night?" one of the uncles shouted.

Maggie jumped and looked at him in alarm. *Wedding night.* Despite the week of planning and her visit to the gynecologist, she hadn't allowed herself to think about the inevitability of this night. But now here it was staring her in the face, and she could only muster one feeling: complete and total panic.

CHAPTER 17

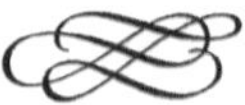

"It was a nice day, I think."

Nick borrowed a car from one of his relatives, and now they were driving to the Jersey Shore for their one night honeymoon. He apologetically told Maggie he was already scheduled to work an event at the park on Sunday evening and couldn't get out of it.

"We'll take a longer trip later," he promised her.

She nodded absently. So far on their journey he was doing all the talking. Her hands were clenched in her lap, and her lips were white from pressing them together.

"Did you have a good day?" he asked.

The uncertainty in his voice registered, and she felt bad. She cleared her throat. "I did. I love your family, Nick."

He smiled at her before turning his attention back to the road. "And they love you. If you knew how very Italian they are you would know how much that means."

"I'm not sure I understand," she said.

"Not many people in my family marry non-Italians," he said. "I've never dated anyone who wasn't Italian."

"I'm sorry," she said sincerely.

He glanced at her. "Why are you sorry?"

She wasn't sure how to tell him she was sorry she had interrupted his life plan. He was supposed to marry some nice Italian girl who loved him. Now he was stuck with her and all her problems.

"Maggie, I'm not sorry. Not at all. I never wanted to marry any of the girls I dated. I wanted to marry you." He reached over and clasped her hand.

She looked out the window and smiled, suddenly shy.

"Your hands are cold. Do you want me to turn up the heat?" he asked.

She shook her head. There was no way to tell him her hands were cold because she was nervous. They had never really kissed and now they were about to… No, she couldn't think of it. One step at a time. The only thing she had to do now was get to the hotel. She would worry about the rest when she arrived.

"Are you happy at your job?"

The abrupt change in conversation caused him to glance at her and jerk the steering wheel slightly.

"What brought that up?"

"Your cousin Alessa."

"My family sticks their nose too far into my business. You probably don't know what that's like, living on a sprawling ranch."

"You're wrong. I live on that ranch with all of my family, and there's nowhere else to go and nothing else to do except be in each others business. Try finding a makeout spot near twenty cowboys who work for your father." Her smile faded as she thought of who she had made out with.

Nick squeezed her hand. "I can't imagine your life."

"I couldn't imagine yours before I experienced it." She paused. "Someday you'll see the ranch."

He smiled. "That sounds nice. I'm anxious to meet your family."

She nodded absently and turned her head to the window again. The question was, would her family be as anxious to meet him, or would they disapprove? She glanced at Nick. She had a difficult time imagining anyone disapproving of him. Still, her family was protective of her. It probably wouldn't sit well that she had married a stranger on a whim.

"Hey, you distracted me," she said suddenly.

He smiled. "It's easy to do."

"Of course it's easy to do. Doesn't mean you should take advantage of my scattered way of thinking."

"You're right," he soothed. "I'm sorry. I wasn't doing it on purpose, though. I think we got sidetracked together. To answer your earlier question, I am happy at my job."

She studied him as he stared straight ahead. Not for the first time she wished she was better at reading people. Kitty could pick things up by tone or expression. Maggie had never been able to do that. She took people for their word and often landed in a heap of trouble because of it. Now she made herself pay attention and try to think like Kitty.

Nick was smiling, but his eyes didn't look happy. His hands were too tight on the steering wheel.

"I'm not sure I believe you," she said slowly. She surprised them both by resting her hand on his leg. "I want you to be happy, Nick."

They reached a stoplight and he turned to look at her. "I am happy, Maggie. Today more than ever." He smiled at her.

She returned it. He gave so much and asked so little in return. A new sort of tension erupted between them as they sat at the stoplight and looked in each other's eyes. As if caught in a trance, she felt herself leaning toward him as he leaned toward her, but before they could reach each other the car behind them honked impatiently.

Nick faced forward again and started to drive. Maggie realized her hand was still on his leg, and now she felt awkward. She removed it and stared straight ahead, too. They finished the remainder of the trip in silence.

Maggie stood nervously in the background while Nick registered for the room, and then she trooped behind him as he carried their bags to their room. It was a lovely room, and at any other time she would have appreciated her first stay in a hotel. Now, however, she was too nervous.

"I'll change my clothes," she said. She took her bag from him and slipped into the bathroom. For a moment she stood over the toilet and debated throwing up. She felt like she could, but then she would have that terrible taste in her mouth, and she didn't want that. Instead she drew out the process of getting ready by taking down her hair, brushing it, scrubbing her face and teeth, and slowly changing her clothes. When at last she emerged she was wearing one of the new nighties she had received at the hastily thrown together shower his cousins held. It was pretty, but not revealing enough to make her uncomfortable. Well, not any more uncomfortable than she already was, anyway.

Nick was lying on the bed in his boxer shorts. He sat up and took in her appearance with awe. She was beautiful. Her figure was perfect and the gown covered enough to make him curious about what was underneath. And then he noticed her eyes looking anywhere but at him.

"Maggie, what's wrong? Are you nervous?"

She nodded.

"Am I making you nervous?" He pointed to himself.

"I've never seen a boy without his clothes on before." She stared at a spot on the curtain.

His mouth opened and his eyebrows rose in surprise. They hadn't talked about it, but he assumed she and Mathew had been together. Despite the fact the girls he dated were from conservative Catholic families few of them were innocent.

"Didn't you and he…" He trailed off.

She shook her head and clasped her hands in front of her.

He realized, belatedly and with no small amount of disappointment, that she wasn't ready for this. She was petrified. To inflict this sort of intimacy on her right now might traumatize her. As much as he hated to postpone a physical relationship with her, he wanted her to be ready for it when it happened.

His t-shirt was lying on the chair. He picked it up and put it on. She looked at him with curious eyes. He perched on the end of the bed and held out his hands to her. She stumbled forward, and he clasped her hands.

"We won't do anything tonight."

"But it's our wedding night," she said.

"And we can set our own agenda," he said. "You're clearly not ready for this. I don't want to push you. We'll go at your pace."

"Y-you're s-so n-nice to m-me," she stammered, and then she started to cry.

"I like you," he said. He pulled her close and tried not to breathe in the scent of her. He placed his hands gently on her back, and quickly moved them when they touched bare skin. *If I survive this torture, I deserve an award,* he thought.

When she finished crying, they sat on the bed to watch television until she started to doze, and then he turned off the set and they fell asleep.

CHAPTER 18

*H*e woke the next morning long before she did. He couldn't say he felt regret, because he didn't. Maybe the right word was remorse. He felt remorse for all that could be between them but wasn't.

Beside him Maggie was curled into a small, protective ball. He longed to put his arms around her and kiss her. Or, at the very least, he longed to push her hair off her face and tell her he loved her. He wanted to promise her everything would be all right, but the truth was, at this moment, he wasn't sure it would. He had married her because he loved her and wanted to take care of her, but why had she married him? There was only one reasonable answer, and it made him sad. She married him because she had no one else. What should have been a happy, exciting first morning of their new life together was instead awkward and uncomfortable as she woke up and caught him looking at her.

"Hi," she whispered.

She smiled, and his doubts fled. For better or worse she was his now. He loved her, and he would make things work between them.

"Hi," he said softly. They shared a smile. He wondered what she was thinking. It occurred to him to ask her, but he was always wary of doing too much or saying too much that might scare her and push her away. The irony of the situation wasn't lost on him. He had been something of a ladies' man. Now he was insecure and uncertain about how to proceed, and the girl in question was his wife.

Tentatively she reached out and clasped his hand. He looked at her in surprise.

"I'm an affectionate person."

"You've never been affectionate with me," he said.

Her smile was wry. "I didn't want you to think I was chasing you."

"Chase me." He said it so enthusiastically that she giggled.

He smiled and allowed himself the luxury of brushing her hair away from her face. Her smile fled. "Does this bother you?"

"No," she said. Disturbed was a better description. Her scalp tingled where his fingers touched, and she didn't understand the sensation. They lay looking at each other in silence for a few minutes. He was very handsome, she thought for the thousandth time. She had always secretly liked dark hair and dark eyes on a man, although she had never told Mathew because he had light blond hair and crystal blue eyes. In her mind's eye she was used to seeing fair-haired babies. Changing the mental image to dark-headed little ones was going to take some time.

"How many kids do you want?" she blurted and blushed when he looked at her in shock.

"That was probably the last question I was expecting this morning," he said.

She felt guilty about last night, and her face flamed again.

He captured a tendril of her long hair and wound it around his finger. "Three seems like a good number." He had never given the matter much thought before he met her. Children had seemed a lifetime away. The thought they might now only be a few years away made his heart beat fast with anticipation. "What about you?"

She shook her head. "You don't want to know."

He smiled. "Now I have to know."

"Six," she murmured.

"Six?" he repeated. He sat up slightly. "Are you sure you're not Catholic?"

"Only by marriage," she said. She touched her finger to the tip of his nose. She couldn't believe she, Maggie Chapman, was flirting.

Nick couldn't believe it either, if the look he was giving her was any indication. He didn't understand her happy mood this morning. He wasn't complaining about it, though. He liked her this way. Since he had known her she had been in mourning. Maybe their marriage was helping her move on.

But it wasn't. Not yet, anyway. The grief came in waves. Sometimes first thing in the morning she was able to suspend reality for a few minutes before it all came crashing down on her. As her early morning euphoria wore off she remembered where she was and why. She was married. To Nick, not to Mathew. Mathew was gone forever, and it was her fault.

Nick watched the play of emotions on her face and then watched it close up completely. It hurt, and he was surprised because it had never hurt before. He understood she was still in love with Mathew. Why should it suddenly start to bother him? *Because now she's my wife.* He understood now why his mother had tried to warn him and what she had meant. The covenant of marriage put an entirely new spin on their relationship. He hadn't realized how different it would feel to be married to her and have her be in love with another man.

A pall settled over them. Maggie knew she was being unfair to Nick by mourning over the life and love she had lost, but she didn't know how to stop. Nick knew she couldn't help it and felt guilty for resenting her.

"What do you want to do today?" he asked at last.

"Can we go to the ocean?" she asked. "I've never seen the Atlantic before."

"Sure."

"And can we get room service?"

He smiled at her enthusiasm. "Yes."

"I've never had room service before. It always looks fun on television."

"Have you ever stayed in a hotel before?" he asked.

She shook her head.

"I haven't stayed in many," he admitted. "I've never traveled anywhere."

"I've never traveled anywhere but here. Ranch life doesn't lend itself to vacations. Dad is pretty much on call all the time. I've always wanted to travel more."

"Me, too," he said. "Let's."

She smiled. "All right."

He paused. "Did you and he plan to travel together?"

"No." She wasn't sure why but she and Mathew had never talked about traveling, even though they both had the freedom and the money to do it. The Henshaws were wealthy, and Mathew didn't have much responsibility at his ranch.

Nick smiled, pleased this was something only between the two of them. He hated feeling like a repeat of everything she had already done with Mathew. Or a stand in for everything she wanted to do with him and couldn't.

"Are you all right, Nick?" she asked. She sensed his sadness and had some vague notion she was the cause, which she hated. She didn't want to ever hurt him if she could help it.

"I'm fine," he said. He forced a smile. "Let's order that room service now." He reached across her to the nightstand in order to retrieve the menu. She rolled onto her back so her shoulder wouldn't butt against him, but now they were pressed intimately together, front to front. They froze.

After a few beats he cleared his throat and eased away from her, hoping she didn't notice the sweat beading on his forehead.

"What looks good to you?" he asked.

She scooted close in order to read the menu he held aloft. Without conscious thought his arm eased around her and her head rested on his shoulder. It felt nice. Natural.

She pointed to the western omelet. "And juice, please."

"Not a coffee drinker?" he asked.

"Sometimes," she answered. "I'm not an addict."

"I am. It's a rule if you're a cop. Working the night shift was brutal." The way he said it didn't sound like he minded, though.

"Tell me about what it was like," she said. Besides their sheriff who was a friend of her father, she didn't know anyone who was in law enforcement.

He placed their food order and started to tell her some stories of his days on the beat.

"What does that mean, the beat?" she asked.

"It's the patrol area you walk. Rookies start on the beat. It's not a desirable job, believe me." He continued to talk. She snuggled down into his embrace and listened with rapt attention. Distractedly he began to sift his fingers through her hair, and she started to experience the tingling feeling again. Only now it was spreading to the rest of her. She froze and grasped his t-shirt with her fingers.

He paused in the middle of his story. "Are you all right? Are you ill?"

She shook her head. She knew she was reacting to him, but she didn't know why. Mathew had never had this effect on her. Her mind recalled a conversation she'd had with Kitty when she and Dante first started dating. It was around the time Maggie and Mathew first started dating, and Kitty asked what it was like to kiss Mathew. Maggie had replied that it was sweet, which it was.

But then Kitty had told her that kissing Dante was like touching a match to a firework. The imagery stayed in her head for days until she finally forced herself to banish it. Kissing Mathew was pleasant, and she determined it was probably the same for Kitty and Dante, only Kitty was better with words than she was.

Now, however, she was looking at Nick and wondering if she had been wrong. Maybe what she and Mathew had was sweet, and that was all it ever would have been. Maybe if she and Nick kissed it would be like a match to a firework. He was still looking at her warily, as if trying to figure out her sudden stillness and introspection. Her hand crept up until her fingers were lightly pressing on his lips. He froze. She didn't. Her fingers edged around to the base of his skull and lightly urged his head toward hers. Even with Mathew she had never been so brazen, but she was driven by curiosity and whatever sensation he was awakening in her.

He shifted his position so she was lying flat on the bed with his arm resting beside her, supporting his weight, and the other hand twined in her hair to draw her close. Once they were settled he slowly descended toward her, and then a sharp rap on the door shattered the moment. Maggie self-consciously covered herself with the sheet as Nick went to answer the door and tip the hotel employee.

When he returned to her they ate on the bed in silence. He wondered if she was upset, but then she held out a bite of her omelet for him to taste.

As for him, he was anything but upset; he was elated. After last night's shyness and fear, he thought it would take months to build up to some sort of physical relationship, and then this very morning she tried to kiss him. He chewed slowly while he thought that over. Maybe that was the key. Maybe he had to let her make the first moves so she could maintain her comfort level. He nodded slightly as he came to a decision. That was the answer, for sure. If they were ever to progress in their marriage then Maggie had to be the one to make all the moves.

Maggie, on the other hand, misunderstood his thoughtful silence. She had never been so forward with a man before, and she thought she must have offended him, especially when he made no move to reinstate their interrupted kiss. She was embarrassed and vaguely ashamed, despite the fact that he was now her husband. She vowed that from now on she wouldn't be the one to pursue him. If he wanted to move forward from where they were, then he would have to be the one to make all the moves.

CHAPTER 19

After breakfast they spent a few hours walking the beach, and then they went home. A new sort of silence hovered between them now, and Maggie didn't understand it. It was almost like Nick was waiting for her to do something, but she didn't know what she was supposed to do. Walking the beach had been nice. It was too late in the season for sunbathing, but there were still girls there in bikinis, and more than one of them looked at Nick with interest. He didn't seem to notice, but Maggie was still unhappy. She wished he would take her hand or put his arm around her, but he didn't, so they walked together in thoughtful silence.

Nick didn't notice the girls at the beach, but he did notice the other couples. They looked happy, he thought. Settled. In love. It was a stark contrast to Maggie and himself who walked almost three feet apart, each lost in thought. He so badly wanted to hold her hand or put his arm around her, but he was reluctant to scare her off and erase any ground they had gained that morning.

Arriving home did nothing to erase the awkwardness. Maggie wondered if Edda could sense what they hadn't done on their honeymoon. Nick felt awkward over what his mother assumed they *had* done on their honeymoon. Edda went out and Nick left soon after to cover security at an event in the park.

Maggie felt listless and restless all at the same time. She didn't want to stay in the tiny apartment, and she hadn't eaten supper, so she walked to the deli down the street. She ordered a sandwich and sat at a table in a corner to eat it.

"You're Nicky's new girl, aren't you?"

Maggie looked up to see a girl staring at her with a cold, belligerent glare.

"I'm his wife," Maggie corrected. She wasn't sure where her newfound courage came from. Usually confrontation sent her running away in tears, but something about this girl rubbed her the wrong way. "And who are you? Another cousin?" she asked with some hesitancy. She hoped not.

"I'm his old girl," the girl said. She tipped her chin defiantly.

"Oh." Maggie said. She wasn't sure how to respond. Nick had never told her about any of the girls he dated.

The girl was staring at her like she was waiting for her to comment further. Maggie put down her sandwich with a sigh.

"He didn't tell you about me?" the girl pressed.

"No," Maggie said.

"He should have. We were serious."

"What's your name?" Maggie asked. She didn't care, but obviously the girl wasn't going to go away. She might as well know who she was talking to.

"Angelina."

Maggie nodded and attempted to return to her sandwich. "Was there something further you needed?" Maggie asked.

Angelina continued to look down her nose at her. "You're not Italian, you're not Catholic, and you're not even that pretty. I'm trying to figure out what he sees in you."

Maggie blinked at her, taken aback by her frank hostility. Several retorts ran through her mind, but she refrained. Maybe in different circumstances Angelina was nice. After all, Maggie would most likely be hurt and angry if her boyfriend suddenly married someone else.

"What's done is done," she said at last. She wouldn't apologize to this rude girl when she didn't know Nick's side of things.

"If you think it's over, you're wrong," Angelina said. "Nicky is too much a part of us to ever belong to you. One day soon he's going to come to his senses, and I'll be right here waiting with open arms." Her statement sounded even more menacing because of her sharp, tough-sounding accent.

"Maybe you could be his date at my funeral because the only way you're getting to my husband is over my dead body," Maggie said. Once again she was surprised at herself. She didn't know she had it in her to say such a thing, and she had no idea she was a jealous person.

Angelina raised an eyebrow at her. Everywhere she went people told her what a sweet pushover Nicky's new wife was. She wondered if this was the same person everyone else had met. She left the restaurant, confused.

Strangely, the confrontation made Maggie hungry. She finished her sandwich and ordered another. She hadn't had much of an appetite since Mathew died. It was nice to enjoy food again, although she would have to be careful or the inactivity of city life would make her gain weight. She rolled her eyes. If she gained so much as one ounce, she knew everyone in the neighborhood would say she was pregnant. She chuckled to herself because she realized she felt very much at home here.

Maggie tried to wait up for Nick, but Edda told her he sometimes didn't get in until the wee hours of the morning. She went to their now shared bedroom and made a valiant effort to stay awake but fell asleep almost as soon as her head hit the pillow.

The next morning a small sound woke her, and she opened her eyes to see Nick standing beside the bed already dressed for work.

"Sorry," he whispered. "I didn't mean to wake you."

She sat up. "I'm sorry I couldn't stay up last night and then slept too late this morning."

He sat on the edge of the bed and smiled at her. He loved to see her first thing in the morning with her hair tousled from sleep.

She smiled at him.

Tension hummed between them.

"Was there something you wanted to talk to me about?" he asked.

She had missed him last night and wanted to see him for that reason alone, but maybe he felt she needed a reason to try and wait up for him. "I met a friend of yours last night," she blurted.

His eyebrows rose. "Oh? Who?"

"Angelina." She studied his face carefully for a reaction. What she saw surprised her. He looked afraid.

"Did she do anything to you?"

"No," she drawled.

He let out a relieved breath. "Angelina is…temperamental."

"So I gathered," Maggie said wryly. "She made it sound like I came between you."

"She would," Nick said irritably.

Maggie reached over, clasped his hand, and brought it to her lap. "Nick, if that's the case I'm very sorry. I didn't know you were seeing anyone."

He smiled, so delighted by the physical gesture he wanted to do a little dance. Instead he moved slightly closer and rested his free hand on the bed near her thigh. "Angelina and I grew up together, kind of like family. We dated off and on, mostly when I wasn't seeing anyone else. I'm sorry to say I sort of used her when no one else was available, and she may have gotten the impression my feelings for her are deeper than they are. She's a friend from the neighborhood, and that's all."

"Oh." She didn't know why his words should cause her heart to flutter with delight, but they did.

He let out a breath. "I wish I could stay, but if I don't go now, I'm going to be late, and the guys will bust my chops about the reason." He wagged his eyebrows at her and she blushed.

"Oh," she said again. "Have a good day then." She wondered if he would kiss her and half hoped he would. He hesitated in front of her for what felt like a long time, squeezed her hand, and left.

"Aren't husbands supposed to kiss their wives?" she muttered. In a rare fit of temper, she picked up his t-shirt from his side of the bed and flung it at the door.

That night when he returned home, Edda was working late, so they ordered a pizza.

"It's ridiculous to have to eat take out every time your mother is away," she told him. "I need to learn to cook."

"Mmm, hmm," he said. He had been watching her with a funny sort of smile since he walked in the door.

She set aside her pizza and wiped her fingers on a napkin. "Why are you looking at me that way?"

He set aside his pizza, too. "The first rule of the neighborhood is that there are no secrets here."

"So?" she asked.

"So everyone knows exactly what you said to Angelina last night."

She mentally reviewed the conversation. "What did I say that was so bad?"

"Nothing." He could barely contain his laughter, and she noticed.

"Are you going to tell me?" she asked irritably. He had no idea she had a temper, and he was tempted to keep her in suspense; but he was also bursting at the seams, so he said it all in one breath.

"You told her she could have me over your dead body."

"What's so unusual about that? She had it coming."

"That's what's so unusual. She's had it coming for years, but no one had the nerve to give it to her. Then you, my sweet little flower of a wife, let her have it with both barrels." He grinned at her, so pleased with her jealous display that he could kiss her into oblivion.

Maggie liked the way he called her his sweet little flower of a wife. "That's right, I am your wife, and don't you forget it." She tapped his chest with her index finger.

Her caught her hand and kissed it, and Edda walked in the door, cutting off an opportunity for anything more.

CHAPTER 20

The next week Maggie got a job. The downstairs neighbors, the DeLucas, told her about an opening for a secretarial position at a veterinarian's office a few blocks away. Maggie interviewed and the doctor hired her because he liked her, and despite her lack of experience.

At home she and Nick were feeling their way in their new relationship. They didn't fight, but they couldn't seem to progress past their cozy friendship. Nick was afraid of pushing too hard, too fast, and Maggie was afraid of being too brazen. Every night they lay side by side with the strange and intense chemistry buzzing between them. Maggie was finding it more and more difficult to fall asleep, although she didn't tell Nick, and he didn't tell her he was having the same problem. Finally on the fourth day of their marriage she reached a tentative hand to his. Once she felt the reassuring pressure of his hand around hers she fell into a dreamless and comfortable sleep.

She was nervous on the first morning of her new job.

"You're going to do great," Nick said.

"Thank you," she said sincerely. "What should I do with the money?"

"What money?" he asked absently as he put on his shoes.

"The money I make from my new job. I don't know where your bank is."

He sat up in alarm. He realized belatedly they hadn't combined any of their financial information. He hadn't added her to his credit cards, either. She had most likely been using the money her father sent with her months ago, and it had to be near an end now.

"Maggie, I'm sorry," he said. He was so contrite he broke his no touching rule and reached across the bed to pull her into his embrace.

She looked up at him in a daze, more shocked by his touch than by his apology. "Why are you sorry?" She reached a tentative hand up to touch his cheek.

"Because I haven't been taking good care of you."

"You've been taking excellent care of me," she argued.

"I haven't given you a credit card."

She smiled. "I get a credit card?"

"You get everything," he said sincerely. "I'll take care of it today. I'll add you to all of my accounts, and you can put your money in our bank. Or you can keep it; I don't care. I make plenty for the both of us."

She had no idea how much he made or where his money went. She didn't know how much rent they paid for their apartment. Someday she thought it might be nice to have an apartment of their own, but she didn't want to push him if he couldn't afford it.

"I'm going to save my money," she told him. Maybe someday if she saved enough they could buy a house of their own. Then she thought of Montana, and her smile fled. How could she be planning a life and a future away from her home? Was she so fickle she could set up house wherever she landed? Although Nick was her husband, and his home was here. She was suddenly confused and homesick.

"What's that look for?" he asked. He smoothed his thumbs along her shoulders.

She shivered from the new sensation. It felt heavenly. "It's nothing." She didn't want to disrupt this moment with her forlorn thoughts. Instead she slipped her arms around his neck. Her eyes closed, and then he was gone. She opened her eyes and stared at his back while he tied his other shoe.

"You'd better not be late on your first day," he told her. He was sure she had been thinking of Mathew, and he couldn't stand the thought of himself as a stand-in when he was so desperate for her.

"All right."

The soft, injured tone of her voice made him turn around and look at her, but she had her back to him as she reached for her clothes. He sighed. "Have a good day, Maggie. I'll see you tonight."

She nodded but didn't speak again as he left. When he was gone she buried her face in her shirt and took a steadying breath. It had happened again. She threw herself at him, and he was repulsed by her. When would she learn to stop pursuing him? He would come to her when he was ready, if he ever was. She tried hard to put it out of her head so her mind could focus on her work.

Once she arrived, though, she realized it was wasted effort. She was a slow typist. The phone system confused her. The massive amount of callers overwhelmed her. She crashed the computer three times and jammed the printer, all before lunch. The only thing she had going for her was the ease with which she handled the customers. And it was her saving grace. The veterinarian was frustrated up to his eyeballs with her ineptitude, but every patient he saw had a pleasant comment about his new friendly receptionist. He decided to be patient and give her until the end of the week to turn it around.

But she didn't, and she knew it. Every day she messed up worse and worse. She simply couldn't keep things straight in her mind. She picked up the wrong lines on the phone and hung up on people. She scheduled appointments incorrectly and forgot to tell the doctor about cancellations. The most upsetting part to her was that she was trying her hardest and still failing; she had never felt worse about herself. Most people would probably see it as a cake job, but it was too much for Maggie.

Nick and Edda noticed her downcast spirit, but they didn't comment, and she didn't fill them in. It was enough that she was no doubt going to be fired. No need to jump the gun and tell her new family what a failure she was.

On Friday morning she had to make herself go to work and face the music. She didn't need Kitty's observant nature to know she was going to be fired today. Unfortunately, the day was even worse and more hectic than usual because one of the vet techs called in sick. The doctor snapped at her throughout the day. Maggie was almost in tears, and then something happened to make her forget herself completely.

A woman brought in a bull mastiff with an injured paw. The owner, a tiny woman who was weeping uncontrollably, could barely control the huge dog that was snarling and snapping and straining at his leash. Maggie knew he was in pain, and her sudden resolve to help made her temporarily forget the ringing phones and move forward to help.

"Oh, no, don't," the owner pleaded. "He doesn't like strangers, and he's afraid, and…" She stopped talking because Maggie moved her out of the way and took control of the leash. She looked the dog in the eye, told him to sit, and he obeyed. It was she, and not the stunned owner, who led him sedately into the examining room. Apparently the dog was a frequent visitor because the doctor also looked at her in bewilderment.

"Is this dog on tranquilizers?" he asked the owner as soon as she gathered herself together enough to come through the door.

"No," the woman said. "She brought him in." She pointed to Maggie.

Maggie looked at them in confusion, not sure what the fuss was about. She had always had a way with animals. "He's hurt and scared," she said. The doctor took control of the leash and Maggie turned to try and salvage the mess she had made of the reception area. Four lines were ringing and she had no idea which ones she had already talked to.

The woman with the dog left, and Maggie realized the doctor was standing on the other side of the desk staring at her.

"I'm sorry I left the desk. She looked like she needed help."

"She does," he said. "She got that dog from a rescue, and she's never been able to control him. He's bitten everyone in the office and nearly destroyed her home. Today is the only time in two years I have ever seen him calm or behaved."

"Oh," she said. She still wasn't sure if she was in trouble or not. "I've always liked animals."

"Hmm," he said. He reached around the desk, picked up the phone, and turned on the answering service.

"I didn't know the phone could do that," she said.

"I know," he said wryly.

She braced herself for the inevitable, but then he shocked her speechless.

"For the rest of the day you're working with me as my assistant. I need help with my patients more than I need a receptionist today, and I want to test my theory."

She didn't ask him what the theory was. She didn't care. All she heard was that she wouldn't have to try to figure out the horrible phone and, even better, she was going to work with animals. She walked so quickly to his office that she beat him there and then giggled when he sighed in exasperation at her.

That day would go down as one of the best she ever spent. Either she and the doctor worked well together, or she had a natural talent for veterinary medicine because she almost always anticipated his needs before he spoke them. The only time he had to voice a request was when he needed a medical instrument she wasn't familiar with. By the end of the day she was exhausted but happy. For the first time since stepping foot in this office she felt competent. And then the doctor spoke.

"Maggie, I'm sorry to tell you that you are the worst receptionist I've ever had. The bad news is you're fired. The good news is I want to hire you as my new vet assistant. I'll train you, but you'll need to get certified. Your starting pay will be higher than what you're making as a receptionist, and when you're certified you'll get a raise."

Tears filled her eyes and spilled over. "Is this some sort of

Brooklyn humor? You're really going to pay me for working with animals?"

"If you want the job. And if you swear to never, ever touch the phone here again."

"I promise," she said. "Thank you. Thank you so much." She smiled and swiped at her tears. She couldn't wait to tell Nick.

When she walked in the door and Nick saw her tear-streaked face he pulled her into his embrace.

"Baby, I heard the job's not going well. I'm sorry you got fired."

She hadn't told him or anyone else about the misery her job had become, but of course everyone already knew. He was right. There were no secrets here. Then she laughed because for once she had outpaced the neighborhood gossip.

"You haven't heard the best part, though," she said. She moved back, but kept her arms clasped around his waist.

"What?" he asked. He was happy for her already, and the realization made her heart sing.

"I got a new job."

"Already?" he asked. "What is it?"

"Veterinary assistant. And I'm making a few thousand more than my last job."

He picked her up and twirled her around the tiny apartment. "I'm so proud of you."

She laughed delightedly and held on tight. "Thank you. I'm not sure I've ever been this happy." She stopped short because she meant it, and the thought hurt. Wasn't her time with Mathew the happiest she ever was? She felt disloyal, guilty, and confused.

Nick felt the abrupt shift in her mood. Once again when he touched her she fell into a funk. He was sure the reason was because she was mourning Mathew. He found as time went on he minded more, not less. Would he ever be able to outlive Mathew's memory?

Maggie knew she had done something to upset Nick, but she didn't know what.

"Nick, I," she began, but he interrupted her.

"Let's go out to celebrate," he said. He turned and walked out the door without waiting for an answer.

"Celebrate," Maggie whispered. Right now with Nick upset at her it was the last thing she felt like doing.

CHAPTER 21

From that night on things were different between them. Maggie felt like they were moving farther apart instead of closer together, and she was correct. Nick was slowly but surely sealing up a portion of his heart and tucking it away from her. He couldn't continue knowing she was in love with another man and wondering if she was thinking about him when he was with her.

Maggie felt the loss keenly, although she couldn't put a name to it. Nick was still polite and caring toward her, but it wasn't the same. She wanted to fix it, but she didn't know how. So instead she threw herself into her new job and determined to be the best veterinary assistant ever. She quickly and easily passed her certification and became a voracious reader on the subject of veterinary medicine.

When she wasn't busy at work she was busy learning to cook. Edda was teaching her how to cook Italian food, and Maggie was blossoming. She made her first marinara and proudly held out the spoon so Nick could have a taste.

"Delicious," he declared.

She set the spoon aside and hugged him around the neck. "Now you'll have to repeat that at the family gatherings because I plan to enter the competition." She kissed his cheek and left him smiling after her when she entered the kitchen.

That weekend he went out without her.

After watching her stew in misery for an hour, Edda told her the name of his favorite hangout and sent her with the instructions to, "Make him take you next time."

Maggie spent some time getting ready before she went. One thing she had learned was that New York fashions were different than Montana fashions, and the clothes she owned looked strange here. Since she was earning her own money she had recently ventured out to buy a few new items. She put on one of her new outfits tonight and left her hair down around her shoulders. Nick had mentioned once he liked it that way, and it was a change from her usual French braid or ponytail. She applied some makeup and surveyed herself in the mirror. She looked like a native, she thought, and she looked pretty, even if she wasn't Italian or Catholic.

Nick's hangout was a trendy-looking club called *Bobby's*. She thought it might be a cop hangout because many of the men outside had that cagey, suspicious look Nick wore whenever he was in a crowd. She realized how well she knew him now, and she smiled. In some ways he truly felt like her husband; every way but the most important, but she wouldn't think of that now.

"Hey, sweetheart, are you old enough to be here?" the man at the door asked her. She fished for her identification, glad she had remembered to bring it.

The man looked at it and then at her. "Are you related to Nicky?" he asked.

She nodded. "He's my husband."

"Hey, I didn't know Nicky was married," he said, smiling. "Congratulations."

She gave him a tight smile. For all she knew he was a complete stranger to Nick, but it still annoyed her Nick hadn't told him he was married. "Any idea where he's sitting tonight?"

"He's at his regular table over there," the guy pointed to a large table in the corner.

Maggie saw Nick and smiled; but when she saw who he was sitting with him her smile died. There was a large group of guys, but right next to Nick sat Angelina.

"Thank you," Maggie said to the man.

He watched her go with a smile. Maybe that explained why Nicky looked so happy every time he saw him lately.

Although, he wasn't happy tonight. He was miserable and missing Maggie like crazy. He didn't want to be away from her, but he had to for his sanity. Night after night they lay there like strangers when it was the opposite of what he wanted. And then she was always busy with her job or with his mother in the kitchen. He never saw her anymore, and when he did he had to wonder if she was seeing Mathew when she looked at him.

When he looked up and saw her he thought he was imagining things. And when he saw the look of utter anger on her face he knew he had to be. His Maggie had never been angry with him. Despite the firm set of her lips and her narrowed eyes she looked almost as beautiful as she did on their wedding day. She rarely wore her long hair down. She looked like some avenging angel as she descended on him. He wondered why and then remembered Angelina sitting beside him. Angelina had only shown up a few minutes ago, and he hadn't talked to her more than saying hello. She was busy flirting with the other guys at the table, and he was busy mooning over Maggie. Now Maggie was here, and could it be she was jealous? He smiled at her, but she didn't return it.

"Hello, Nico," she said.

He coughed to cover his laugh. "Margaret," he nodded at her. Then he realized the other guys were looking at her with far too much interest. "Guys, this is my wife, Maggie."

"Your wife," the guys echoed. Nick noted the mixture of awe and envy in their voices with pride and satisfaction.

"Hello," Maggie smiled with some of her usual shyness.

"Join us," one of the guys said.

"Thank you." She looked at Angelina who was on the end, but she made no move to allow Maggie entry. To Nick's utter shock Maggie raised an eyebrow at her and climbed over her. She sat in his lap before sliding down to rest on the other side of him.

"Full of surprises, aren't you Margaret?" he whispered when her ear was close to him.

"You have no idea," she said, and winked in a way that set his mind spinning and his heart racing. She focused on Patrick Kelly, the only guy with red hair at the table. "You're not Italian, either, huh?"

He smiled. "No, but I'm Catholic. Sorry."

"Maggie's Catholic, too," Nick said. "By marriage."

Maggie had never been able to stay angry at anyone for long, least of all Nick, whom she had missed sorely. She turned to him with a smile and pressed her palm to his cheek. The contact only lasted for a second, not enough to draw attention or seem conspicuous, but Nick and Maggie felt like they were suspended in time. A shock ran from her hand to his face and back again, and they communicated something with their eyes they had never said with their lips; they were deeply attracted to each other. Maggie dropped her hand and he put his arm around her. She moved imperceptibly closer to him and rested her hand on his leg.

"I've never seen you guys in the park," Maggie said. "Are you from the fifth precinct?"

The guys nodded their assent. Nick was surprised by Maggie's perception. She wasn't one for details. The realization that she had paid close attention when he talked about himself warmed his heart, which was already beating a staccato rhythm.

"What secrets can you tell me about my husband?" Maggie asked them.

"I could tell you some secrets," Angelina said suggestively.

Maggie turned cool eyes on her. "I'm sure you could tell me secrets about a lot of men. I only want to hear about Nick." She turned her back to her and focused on the men. She was as surprised as they were by her words. She had never been catty before, but then she never had to be. For her whole life there was only her and Mathew with no competition. The only other girls she had ever known were her sisters, and she would certainly never be jealous of them. But somehow seeing Angelina sidled up next to *her* husband with possessiveness made every angry and protective instinct she possessed rise to the surface.

"Where to begin," one of the guys said. Maggie realized later she never did hear their names. "First off, did he ever tell you why his nickname was Teddy Bear?"

Nick groaned. "Not that one," he said.

Maggie pressed her hand over his mouth and laughed. "Definitely that one," she said. "Start there and keep going. We've got all night."

CHAPTER 22

The conversation at the table almost did last all night. It was well after midnight when Maggie and Nick finally said their goodbyes. At some point during the evening, Angelia slunk away so Maggie didn't have to deal with her any more. But she had almost forgotten her because she was having so much fun talking to the other guys. They spent a long time detailing story after story for her, and a new picture of Nick started to emerge. This one was Nick the Cop, and it was a revelation. She knew he was protective of her, but the man they described was a fearless leader who kept a cool head in any situation and was an asset in a crisis. He was also very funny. They told her a few stories about his interactions with some less than savory criminals, and she laughed until she had tears in her eyes. After they finished telling her about Nick, they wanted to know about her and seemed fascinated by what she told them. None of them had ever been out west before, and ranches and cowboys were mythical to them.

"I look forward to meeting your wives next time," Maggie said as the evening came to a close.

"So do we," the red-haired one said with a wry smile.

"None of you is married?" Maggie asked.

"No," the guy said. "And we all thought we would beat Nick to the altar. You cost us some money in lost bets, Maggie." He smiled to let her know he was teasing.

"Why didn't you think Nick would get married?" she asked. "He's a perfect husband. I can't imagine anyone else more marriageable."

That sent the guys into peals of laughter, but she never received an answer to her question because Nick put an arm around her waist and lifted her out of the seat. "All right, wife, you've learned enough about me for one night," he said. He nodded to his friends. "See you guys, if I decide to ever speak to you again after this night of humiliation."

"You can stay home next time," Kelly said. "Just send Maggie." He grinned at Nick's inevitable reaction.

"To quote my wife, 'Over my dead body.'" He gave them another upward nod and dragged Maggie away.

Once they were outside the club, the atmosphere between them was tense. It wasn't an angry tension, but it still unnerved them.

"I like your friends," Maggie said. The edginess between them was about to make her babble. "They seem nice, and they're funny." She relived some of the highlights of the evening and didn't allow him a chance to speak until they arrived home. When she started to open the door he put a hand out to stop her.

"Why did you come for me tonight?" he asked. His voice was calm, but inside he was in turmoil. Tonight was a glimpse at what they could have together, if only there wasn't the ghost of another man between them.

"I didn't like being left behind tonight," she said. "Especially with no explanation. And then I got to the club and that girl was there."

Her pretty face puckered into a frown. At any other time he would have smiled, but he was too keyed up. "That's it then? You felt left out and jealous?"

She stared at his chest. "I missed you, Nick." She chanced a glance into his eyes and was encouraged by what she read in them. "I feel like I haven't seen you lately with my job. And it also seems like you've been angry at me, like you're pushing me away."

He didn't know he had been so blatant in pushing her away. He meant to protect himself, not hurt her. She had opened up; now it was his turn. "Sometimes it's difficult for me, knowing I'm second place."

Her mouth opened slightly and her breath came out in a puff. For the first time she saw things from his point of view. No wonder he was avoiding her; it must be terribly painful to view Mathew as his competition.

"I'll tell you a secret I've never told anybody," she said. She leaned against the wall behind her and pressed her palms to his chest. "Before Mathew, I used to dream about the guy I would marry someday. He was always tall," she paused because he grimaced. He was five foot ten, which might not seem tall to him, but she was only five foot four, so he was tall to her. "Taller than me," she amended, and he relaxed. "And he always had dark hair, dark eyes, and a dark complexion." Her index finger traced lazily over his face.

He took a small step forward and smiled. His hands settled on her waist, and she clutched at his shirt. "If I'm hearing you correctly, you're saying I'm your dream guy."

"Yes, but there's one small difference between you and the guy from my dreams."

"What?"

She swallowed, forcing herself to be brave and say what she was thinking. "The guy in my dreams kissed me."

"Then by all means let me oblige, Mrs. Marino." He placed one hand on the small of her back and used it to press her further into his embrace. For a moment he hovered in front of her face and looked at her. The small space between them crackled with electricity, and Maggie's hand on his chest trembled. Finally the terrible suspense was over and he touched his lips to hers, softly at first, and then with a blinding intensity that engulfed them.

Briefly Maggie was reminded of the time a spark touched a pile of dry kindling during a drought on the ranch. The resulting fire had been brilliant and intense. That was how she felt now as Nick kissed her, and then kissed her again and again. She couldn't think, she couldn't breathe, but she could *feel*. Nick tried to pull away from her for whatever reason, but she wouldn't let him go. Instead she pulled him impossibly closer. He kept one hand on her hip and pressed the other against the wall to support them. Finally he was able to break away enough to speak.

"Maggie, if one of the neighbors opens a door we're going to cause a scandal," he whispered. Then he pressed his lips to her neck and kissed her, and she forgot what he said completely. After what felt like another half hour he broke off again.

"Why do you keep stopping?" she asked. Her lips were swollen and her hair was in a tangled mass, but she didn't care.

Nick smiled. "Because we're about to become indecent in the middle of the hallway, and I know for a fact it's a crime." He kissed her lightly, teasingly. "What do you say we take this inside?" He pulled back and his eyes searched her face.

She returned his solemn stare. Was she ready for what was about to happen? "Yes," she said. The word was weighted because she was answering his question as well as her own. "Let's go to our room." She tipped her face up to kiss him again, but he eluded her.

"Hold that thought," he said. He was laughing at her eagerness and haste when they tripped into the house, and then they froze. His mother was lying on the couch where she had obviously fallen asleep waiting for them. She sat up, and Maggie didn't at first understand the look on her face.

"The police called," she said without any preamble. "Your aunt is in the hospital, Maggie. Someone broke into her apartment and beat her."

Maggie started to shake, and Nick wrapped a reassuring arm around her. "Did they take anything?"

Edda shook her head. "It wasn't a robbery. He wanted to know where you were. He told her his name was Steve and you were his wife."

Maggie missed the last word because a ringing sound entered her ears, and everything went black.

CHAPTER 23

"How did he find me?" Maggie asked. Her faint had been a brief swoon, but Nick and Edda still forced a cloth to her head and made her lie down. Now she was in their bed with Nick beside her. His right arm was tucked securely around her waist and his left arm smoothed the hair off her forehead.

"It could have been through public records. He probably searched for relatives. It would be the logical place to start."

Her eyes opencd with renewed panic and her hand on his arm became a claw. "Marie," she whispered. Marie was her aunt in Oregon, her father's sister who had five young children. If he hurt Marie, he could have hurt the children, too.

"My guess is he started with Victoria," Nick said soothingly. "He would know New York was a better place to hide you than Oregon."

She nodded in relief that turned to guilt. Guilt because she was glad it had been Victoria instead of Marie, and guilt because she caused it all in the first place. Her eyes flooded with tears. "I need to see her."

"Out of the question."

"Nick, she's in the hospital because of me. I'm her only relative here. I have to go."

"No, Maggie, absolutely not. He could be watching the hospital. He could follow you."

She said the only thing she hoped would convince him. "He might already know where I am. I have to see her to find out what she told him."

"I'll see her. I'll find out, and I'll give her any message you want." He removed the washcloth and pressed a kiss to her now cool forehead. "Baby, you have to realize how serious this is."

"I do," she said. She pressed her palm to his cheek. "Please believe me when I tell you I do, but I *have* to see her. I need to apologize to her. Please, Nicky, please."

He couldn't resist her when she looked at him like that, even if it was a huge risk. "I suppose it's no use having a policeman for a husband if I can't figure out a way to protect you." He stroked his fingers along her cheek. "All right. I'll figure something out. Can I get you anything?"

She shook her head. Belatedly she remembered what the tragedy had interrupted between them. She sat up and pressed a light kiss to his lips. "Do you honor rain checks?"

He grinned at her, knowing the terrible shock had temporarily knocked any amorous thoughts from her head. "As long as you have two forms of identification."

She giggled. "You're cute, Nick."

Despite the trauma of learning Steve found her, she slept soundly and didn't dream. Most likely it was because Nick's arms were around her the whole night. When she woke she was still glued to him and her head was buried in his chest.

"I slept," she said with no small amount of surprise.

"I'm glad." He smoothed his hand along her hair. The feeling was vaguely familiar in a dreamlike way, and she wondered how long he had been doing it.

"Did you sleep?"

"Not much," he admitted. He was worried about her. He didn't think he had ever been more afraid. That psycho had tracked her to New York. He might have gotten it from Victoria who she was married to and that she now lived in Bensonhurst. All the guy would have to do is mention Nick's name in the neighborhood and anyone would tell him exactly where he lived. What if he was outside right now, waiting for his chance at Maggie? He shuddered.

"Cold?" Maggie asked. She pulled the blanket up around him.

"No," he said. They had to see Victoria as soon as possible to figure out what she might have told him. "I have a plan for visiting your aunt." He let her go, propped himself on one elbow, and filled her in on the details.

Less than an hour later they were ready, which was sort of amazing, considering the amount of people involved in the plan. They borrowed clothes and a wig from Mrs. Esposito.

"She wasn't happy you knew she wore a wig," Maggie said.

"She'll get over it," Nick said. "If he's watching the hospital he'll be looking for someone young. Remember what I told you about your walk."

She nodded and reminded herself to walk slowly and hunched. It wasn't comfortable. When they arrived she saw the guys she had met last night stationed around the hospital, but she didn't acknowledge them. Nick had seemingly called every cop he knew to help him with surveillance. He even called his work and had a picture made of Steve from the warrant. Since it was a nationwide warrant for murder, there were no jurisdictional boundaries, and they would be able to arrest him if he was located. Despite all the provisions, Maggie felt vulnerable as she made her way to her aunt's room. She imagined Steve watching her from some hidden spot, and she shivered. What if he tracked her to Bensonhurst? What if he hurt Edda, or Mrs. Esposito, or one of the DeLuca children in his mad pursuit of her? She forced her mind from the topic as she pushed open the door.

She stood in the doorway and fought back tears. There was no love lost between them, but she wouldn't wish her worst enemy to be in this condition. Her aunt's face was unrecognizable through the cuts and bruises.

"It's not as bad as it looks," Victoria murmured through stiff lips that barely moved.

"If it's even a little bit as bad as it looks, then it's awful," Maggie said. She came near and sat beside the bed. "I'm so sorry, Victoria."

"It's not your fault," Victoria said. Maggie was touched by the sincerity and softness in her tone. She peered behind her niece to the door. "You can tell your friend to relax out there. I didn't tell the psycho anything, not your friend's name or the fact that he lived in Bensonhurst. I told him you ran away from home and didn't change my story."

Maggie could well imagine how badly Steve beat her to get her to change her story. "I'm so sorry," she repeated again. "And I also have to tell you Nick is my husband now." She wiggled her ring finger half-heartedly.

Victoria tried to gasp, and then coughed and winced. "Husband," she repeated hoarsely. "Oh, this is all my fault."

"It is not," Maggie argued. "It's my fault. I'm the one he was after."

"No, not that," Victoria said. "This," she waved weakly at Maggie's hand. "I pushed you at that boy. I pushed you into marriage at eighteen when it was what I was trying so hard to prevent." She closed her eyes on a wave of pain.

"It's all right," Maggie told her. "Nick is a good guy. I'm very happy with him." She smiled when she realized she meant it. "Some people are designed for grand things. I'm not. I'm a simple country girl whose dream in life was to be married and raise a family. And there's nothing wrong with that," she added firmly.

Victoria smiled, or tried to. "Believe it or not I used to be like you. Shocking, I know. I was young and sweet and full of ideals. Then my parents died. Your mom was married by then. She tried to convince me to move to Montana, but I thought she was crazy. I wanted to be where the action was, so I moved here. I wanted to make it on my own, and I did, but at the loss of my innocence. I had to struggle for everything I ever got. One by one my dreams died, and I turned into the person you see before you. When I finally met my husband, he tried to take everything I had worked for my whole life, so I kicked him to the curb." She sighed. "I saw so much of myself in you when you showed up here. I thought if I helped you toughen up you wouldn't learn things the hard way like I had to. I guess I didn't realize what a trauma you had been through. I thought your father was exaggerating when he said a crazy man was after you."

Maggie couldn't help but smile. "You must not know my father well if you thought he would exaggerate. He's the most straight-laced, straightforward person alive." She paused and swallowed hard. "The man who did this to you killed my fiancé in front of me. I'm so glad you survived. I'm sorry this happened."

"Not your fault," her aunt said. Maggie wondered if she was on medicine that made her sleepy because she was fading quickly. "Maybe when this is all over we could have lunch," she whispered. "My treat."

"I would love that, but it can be my treat. I owe you, and I got a job." She didn't get to tell her aunt what the job was because she fell asleep as soon as she heard Maggie agree to lunch. Maggie studied her a minute longer, gently squeezed her hand, and let herself out of the room.

CHAPTER 24

Nick was on edge for the next few days as he waited for the other shoe to drop. Neither he nor any of his fellow police officers spotted any sign of Steve at the hospital, but that didn't mean he wasn't there. Absently Maggie noted an increased police presence in their neighborhood for the next week, and she knew it was because word had spread about her stalker. The neighborhood rallied and vowed to keep a sharp eye for any strangers. A part of Maggie thought it was funny they were in the midst of one of the most populous places in the United States, and yet a stranger still stuck out like a sore thumb. Mrs. Esposito was especially outraged when she learned the story.

"I'd like to see him try to get past me," she said, and then violently shook her bony little fist.

Maggie shuddered as she pictured what would happen if Steve did try to get past the old woman. Every day her guilt and anxiety increased, not for herself, but for all the people she knew and loved. Libby's baby was due any day, or had already been born, and she was missing it. What if something had happened to one of them? What if that's how Steve found out where she was? Had he tortured one of them into talking?

Nick noted her new listlessness with concern. Selfish though it was, he had hoped they turned a corner in their relationship and could move forward. But with the reemergence of her stalker, she seemed to draw further into herself. She wasn't the type of person to become depressed, and he was deeply worried about her. She had also started having nightmares. She whimpered and twitched in her sleep until he wrapped her up tightly with his body, and then she calmed down. And then he was stuck awake, yearning for the girl he was holding like a second skin.

The constant sleeplessness and tension were making them both irritable. They tried not to take it out on each other, but in the end there was no one else. They were together every minute when they weren't working because Nick feared for her safety too much to leave her alone.

One evening Edda was working overtime. She had worked over a lot lately, and Maggie secretly wondered if it was to avoid the tension in the apartment.

"Do you want to get Chinese tonight?" Nick asked as he entered the kitchen where she was preparing supper.

"No, I'm cooking," she said. Her hair was coming loose from its confines and sticking to her sweaty face.

"Leave it," he said. "We'll get take-out." He hated to see her so worn and frazzled.

"I'm halfway done." She set aside the can of tomatoes she was opening. "I know I don't cook as well as your mom, but I thought I've been getting better."

"Maggie, you're fine. But I know you're tired, and I thought it would be easier."

She continued as if she hadn't heard him, which she hadn't because she was having a mental meltdown. "I can't do anything for you like a real wife, at least let me cook for you." She used the back of her hand to push the hair off her face.

"All right," he said. At this point he would agree to anything if it made her feel better. "Is there anything I can do to help you?"

"No," she said wearily. "I can do this. Go relax; I know you're exhausted."

"All right," he repeated. He backed out of the room, keeping a wary eye on her. The strain was showing in her face, and he was more worried about her than ever. He sat on the couch and tuned to the sports network on television. He was drifting off when he heard soft sobs coming from the kitchen.

He sprang up in alarm and looked around to make sure there was no danger. Everything was normal, so he figured the problem must be with Maggie herself. He strode to the kitchen and saw her standing at the sink holding a paper towel around her bleeding thumb. She was crying great streams of tears.

"Honey, what happened?" He gingerly took her hand in his, expecting to see a gruesome cut. But when he removed the towel he saw a small, neat slice. He turned questioning eyes to her face.

"I can't do this anymore," she said between sobs.

His heart froze and his stomach dropped. "Can't do what?" He thought they were happy together, in their way.

"I can't go on living my life in fear, checking behind every door and in every closet, jumping at every little sound. The worst part is knowing that the people around me might get hurt, and some already have. Oh, Nick." She threw her arms around his neck and pressed her face to his chest.

He held her for a long time, and smoothed his hand over her hair. In the night when she had nightmares it was one sure way to relax her.

"Dinner," she said. The sound was muffled because her face was still pressed to his chest.

"I'll finish dinner," he told her. "Sit."

She sat at the tiny table that was barely big enough for the three of them. They could probably fit six of this kitchen into her kitchen in Montana, but she thought maybe she preferred it this way with Nick brushing her knees as he topped the pasta with cheese and stuck it in the oven. He was incredibly handsome. And he was hers. That thought alone was enough to bring a smile to her reluctant face.

"Feeling better?" he asked. He set the timer on the oven and glanced at her out of the corner of his eye.

"You're a good man, Nick," she said sincerely.

He wasn't sure how to take that coming from her. "Some people used to think I was something of a bad boy."

"Girls you dated?" she guessed.

He nodded. He was still standing over her while she sat at the table. He held his hand out to her. She took it and followed him a few feet into the small living room. When he sat she surprised him by settling comfortably into his lap.

"Tell me about the girls you dated," she said. She smoothed her hand over his chest.

He took a deep breath. "Are you sure you want to hear this? Your jealousy seems to get the better of you sometimes."

She smiled against his chest. "I didn't know I was jealous. It's never happened to me before."

"You weren't jealous of him?" He wasn't sure when he had stopped saying Mathew's name, but somewhere along the way it became painful to do so.

"No." She didn't add there had been no reason to be jealous of Mathew. In their world it was only the two of them. She was glad she refrained from telling him when he smiled. It made her sad he felt second best to Mathew. Some day soon she would have to figure out a way to prove to him he wasn't. "The girls," she prompted.

"Right, the girls," he said. He captured her hand and twined their fingers together. "There were lots of girls. Lots." He smiled again when her fingers tensed and tightened on his.

"How many, precisely?"

"I'm not sure I could count that high." She bent his fingers back and he laughed. "I could estimate. Hmm." He stared at the ceiling while he did a mental calculation. "If you count all the girls I ever took out or made out with then the number is over a hundred. If you only count the girls I actually considered girlfriends then the number drops to around two dozen."

He was most likely waiting for her jealousy to bubble over, which it almost did before she was able to put a cap on it. She squeezed her eyes shut tight and tried not to picture all the pretty faces of the many Italian girls he had kissed. "And how many were you, um, intimate with?"

"Three," he surprised her by saying. She thought the number would be much higher since he was known as a playboy. "Catholic guilt goes a long way in staving off those types of relationships for me. My mom wanted me to wait for marriage, but since I didn't plan to be married until I was thirty I didn't think it was possible." He paused. "Now I wish I had waited for you."

She smiled up at him and kissed the tip of his chin. "Why didn't you want to get married until you were thirty?" she asked absently. He slid his hand to the base of her skull and made a circle with his thumb. It was becoming difficult to think.

"Because in all the girls I dated I never once found what I was looking for," he said.

She swallowed hard and stared at his lips as she asked the next question. "What were you looking for?"

"You," he said, and then he kissed her.

There was really nowhere for the kiss to go because it started off with such intensity. Edda might be home any moment, and that knowledge added an element of intrigue to an already explosive situation.

Maggie felt like she was starving for his touch, and he must have felt the same way because there was no slowing down in the steady progression of events between them. The first few times the telephone rang Maggie thought the sound was in her head because she felt like she was imploding. Finally, reluctantly, Nick broke off the kiss and fumbled for the phone.

"Hello," he snapped, and then his tone mellowed. "Yes, Mrs. Esposito. We'll turn it off. Thank you. No, I'm not sure how we missed it when you heard it so clearly. Thank you."

As he hung up the call Maggie started to hear the other, more insistent buzzing sound coming from the kitchen. She blew out a breath and rested her head on the couch. "How long has the oven timer been going off?" she asked.

"At least five minutes, according to Mrs. Esposito." He briefly rested his forehead on her shoulder before reluctantly peeling away from her to turn off the timer. He took the food out of the oven and tore off the oven mitts. "Where were we?" He left the kitchen and advanced on her.

Her spine tingled in anticipation, and then the key turned in the lock. By the time Edda opened the door Maggie and Nick were in the kitchen sedately setting the table.

Over supper Edda noticed the tension between them and misinterpreted it as a continuation of the tension that had been going on the last few days.

"Maybe it's time for you two to get away on a real honeymoon," she suggested. "You need a break."

Nick thought that over. Maybe if he spirited Maggie away somewhere private they would finally be able to consummate their three-month marriage. He smiled at her, but she dropped her eyes to her plate. He thought it was shyness until she spoke.

"I think that's a great idea, Edda, and I know the perfect place. I think we should go home to Montana."

CHAPTER 25

"Absolutely, positively not," was Nick's first reaction when Maggie told him she wanted to go to Montana. His main reason, and the only one that mattered, was the danger that proposition placed her in.

"I'm tired of running," she told him. "I'm tired of hiding. I miss my family. I miss my animals. I want to see Libby's baby. Please, Nicky, please?"

He thought her eyes must be three inches wide when she pled with him like that. It was like saying no to a baby deer, and once again he couldn't do it. Which was how he found himself on a train headed from Billings to her small Montana town.

Maggie was both excited and apprehensive, and was therefore alternately chatty and pensive. When they reached the tiny town he looked around with some smugness. It wasn't so different from what he pictured. He scanned the horizon and saw several homes with lots of land attached.

"Which one is yours?" he asked.

She pinched his cheek. "You're so cute." She walked to the local mercantile, where she was treated like a celebrity, exclaimed over, and hugged by everyone in attendance, and then she asked for a ride.

"We're taking a ride with a stranger?" he asked with no small amount of concern. His cop instincts were on high alert.

"Not a stranger, a *local*. Several people give rides to the ranchers whenever we disembark the train. It's a good way for them to make extra money." She hadn't been able to call her family to let them know she was coming home because she didn't want to tip Steve off about her visit. "Trust me," she said, and ran a soothing hand down his arm.

He sighed, and she knew she had won.

The man who ended up giving them a ride wasn't a stranger to her after all. He had lived in the town for years and spent the hour-long drive recounting the events of Mathew's murder. He was either oblivious or insensitive to the fact that as he spoke Maggie crawled deeper and deeper into her shell, but Nick wasn't.

"I don't think my wife would like to talk about that day any more," Nick said. He used the tone he had adapted for working with criminals, and the guy actually flinched.

"Sorry," he said repentantly. "Sorry, Maggie," he leaned around Nick to see Maggie. "You always were a sweet little bug. I sure didn't mean to upset you." He sat back and then leaned forward again, this time to look at Nick. "Your wife?" he exclaimed. "But she was with Mathew. They were together for years. Everyone knew they were sweethearts since birth. How did…" He stopped talking when Nick gave him a look that promised to rip his tongue out if he uttered one more word.

The remainder of the drive was made in heavy silence. Maggie rested her head on the window and stared at the passing, familiar landscape. She couldn't believe she had stayed away so long. This land was a part of her, and she had missed it.

Her eyes welled with tears when they turned into their long lane, but she pushed them back. She didn't want her family's first view of her in seven months to be one of her crying like a baby.

Nick paid the farmer who gave them a ride. She guessed maybe Nick said something else to him because the man peeled out like demons were after him.

Her father was the first one to step out onto the porch and in his hand was a shotgun she knew to be loaded. It was a sign the family was still on high alert. Her father saw her and carefully set the gun aside before opening his arms to her.

She ran up the steps and threw herself into his embrace. He picked her up effortlessly and held her in a crushing hug. She started to cry then, but she couldn't help it. She had missed him so much, and she was so happy to see him alive and well. The rest of her family filtered out onto the porch and took turns exclaiming over her and hugging her tightly.

Everyone was home: Kitty, Dante, Anne, and Will. She noted with satisfaction that Libby hadn't delivered her baby yet, although she looked miserable and ready to burst. After the initial greetings were over Nick made a small movement behind her. The entire family turned to look at him as one unit. Maggie ran back down the steps and clasped his hand.

"Everyone, this is Nick Marino. He's a police officer in New York City. More importantly, he's my husband."

Her father picked up the shotgun again, and Libby burst into tears.

"Dad," Maggie said reproachfully. She stood in front of Nick who tried to move her out of the way. "Calm down. Let's discuss this rationally so Nick doesn't think we're a bunch of half-cocked hooligans."

Nick had never heard her use such an interesting colloquialism before. He smiled at her and pinched her waist.

That action, along with the way Maggie was acting, made her family pause and look at the couple. Maggie was different, but not in a bad way. It had been the common fear of all of them she would come back bitter, changed irreparably by the terrible tragedy. She was changed, but for the better, it seemed. There was still the same sweet innocence on her face, but a new maturity went with it. If this man claiming to be her husband was responsible for that change, then maybe they would give him a chance.

Kitty was the first to step forward and offer her hand. "Hello, Nick. Welcome to Montana."

Nick smiled as he shook her hand. He had wondered if he would be able to tell the sisters apart, but based on Maggie's descriptions it was easy. Kitty, he knew, was the studious one. She also had the darkest hair and eyes, and she was the tallest. "Hello, Kitty, or do you prefer Katherine?"

Kitty looked slightly taken aback. "Everyone calls me Kitty," she said.

Except her boyfriend, Dante. Nick knew he called her Kat. "I'm hoping to borrow a gun from you. Maggie tells me you have an amazing collection, and I would feel safer armed."

"Sure," Kitty said. She still looked slightly shell-shocked.

"If you're asking for guns already, you're going to fit in here fine." A tall, sandy-haired man stepped forward and held out his hand.

"You're Will," Nick said.

"What gave it away, my total lack of muscle development or my fancy shoes?" He pointed to his leather loafers.

"Neither. You aren't a cowboy, and you aren't half Spanish."

Libby's husband, Dobbie, was a cowboy, and Kitty's boyfriend, Dante, was half Spanish.

The family was warming to this new addition by the minute, except the oldest sister, Anne, who stood staring at Nick through narrowed eyes. Nick knew she was in her last year of law school and set to one day be a prosecutor. He had faced mafia bosses with less steely reserve, and he couldn't help but smile at her. She was a little thing, even smaller than Maggie. Of the sisters, they looked the most alike, although their personalities couldn't be farther apart.

"You're going to do a background check on me, aren't you?" he asked her.

She didn't smile, but beside her Will laughed. "It would save time if you gave me your social security number," she said. Nick didn't know if she was teasing him. Somehow he didn't think she was.

"You must know I'm Libby," Libby said. "And if you know that then you know I'm about to feed you. Come into the kitchen." She put her arm around him to herd him inside.

"I hate for you to do that in your condition. If you show me where the kitchen is, I would be glad to get it myself."

"There's no stopping her," Dobbie said. "Believe me, I've tried."

"You could try hogtying her," Will suggested.

"How do you think she got in that condition?" Dobbie asked with a suggestive wag of his eyebrows.

Libby whirled on him with her mouth open. "Shane Dobbins," she exclaimed. "And in front of our guest."

"Our new brother-in-law," Dobbie corrected. He moved forward and put both arms around Libby. "He's married, don't forget. The cat's out of the bag for Maggie now."

If anything Libby's embarrassment deepened. "What has gotten into you this evening?"

"This baby won't come out and it's making me a nervous wreck," he admitted. "It's either make jokes or pace like a madman."

"I'm so sorry the fact that I'm almost two weeks overdue is taking a toll on you, dearest," Libby said sarcastically as they resumed their walk to the kitchen.

"I forgive you," Dobbie said sincerely, and then dodged away from his wife before she could deck him.

Nick watched it all with fond amusement. He took Maggie's hand and squeezed it. He thought he was going to like his new family very much.

CHAPTER 26

The next morning Maggie suggested to her father that she and Nick go riding with him.

"Nick needs to get the lay of the land a little bit," she said.

"All right," her father said reluctantly.

Maggie looked at Nick and smiled a conspirator's smile. She had told him the bane of their existence as a ranching family was a city slicker who had no idea how to ride. Nick returned her secret smile. Behind them Libby bustled about the kitchen making breakfast. He felt badly about that. He knew that since Libby married Dobbie she hadn't cooked breakfast for the family, and she was most likely only doing it now for his benefit. When he protested, she waved him away.

"I like to keep busy. Also, Dobbie has been hovering over me like a mother chicken, and if he makes me spend one more day in the house doing nothing I am going to hurt him."

Libby was a year younger than him, but in many ways she reminded him of his mom. Just then the front door opened and Libby froze. "You haven't seen me," she whispered, and waddled out the back door as fast as her large size would allow.

"Woman," Dobbie thundered from the front of the house. "I know you're in here. I told you not to get out of that bed or else." He burst into the kitchen. "Where is she?"

When no one answered, he turned accusing eyes to the perfect stack of waffles on the table. "I know she's been here," he said. "No one makes waffles like my Lib."

"Calm down, son, you're going to rupture something," Matt Chapman said easily. "Sit down and eat. Leave your wife be. Goodness knows she'll have no peace soon enough."

Dobbie sat heavily. "She could go into labor at any moment."

"That's so," Matt said between bites.

"And we might not make it to the hospital so far away."

"That's so," Matt repeated.

Dobbie exhaled loudly and looked at his father-in-law in exasperation.

"Celia made it to the hospital all four times," Matt told him before stuffing another bite of waffle in his mouth.

"And I can deliver her if she doesn't make it," Nick said. "I helped my partner deliver a baby on the Brooklyn Bridge once." He sounded as calm as Matt had. Maggie and Dobbie looked at him in amazement.

"You did?" they said in unison.

"Sure. It was graphic, but not so difficult. Mostly it involves being a good catch, which I am. I played baseball," he added with a wink at Maggie.

She flushed and smiled at him. "You're amazing," she said.

He smiled at her earnest tone, and then because he couldn't help himself he leaned over to kiss the tip of her nose. As far as their physical relationship, they were closer than they had been before, but they were still stuck in neutral. Nick had some suspicion Maggie was waiting until the whole business with her stalker was resolved. He didn't want to pressure her, but, on the other hand, he knew the situation could go on for years with as closely as they were all guarding her. Steve might be a madman, but he was a madman with a strong sense of self-preservation. He wouldn't storm the house when he knew so many able-bodied men were guarding it, not to mention the twenty armed cowboys in the bunkhouse.

Dobbie walked with them to the barn. Nick secretly thought it was probably from a mixture of amusement and curiosity. Maggie retrieved her pony from its stall. The animal pranced happily and whinnied when Maggie hugged her neck.

"I've missed you too, sweetheart," she cooed. The pony pricked its ears and looked for all the world like she understood the loving words.

Maggie selected a horse for Nick.

"Uh, Maggie, are you sure you want that one?" Dobbie said. Nick took that to mean the animal could be spirited, and his guess was correct when the horse backed away from him and shook his proud head.

"I think Nick can handle it," Maggie said confidently.

Dobbie and Matt exchanged a look. Dobbie stepped forward, but before he could offer his assistance Nick swung easily into the saddle and brought the large animal under control.

Maggie smiled at the expression on their faces. "Did I mention Nick is with the mounted police patrol?"

"A city slicker who can ride," Matt said. "Now I've seen everything."

Dobbie grinned happily. "Wait until I tell Will the new guy can ride better than him. He's going to want to dig a hole and crawl into it."

The remaining trio laughed and set off. For Nick the journey was a revelation. He had no idea land could be so vast or so beautiful. In the distance was a lone mountain. A couple of times they saw deer and elk scattered among the thousands of cows. Nick didn't mention he had never seen a cow in real life, let alone an elk. Matt went on to tell him about the more elusive wildlife in the area such as wolves and grizzly bears.

"Have you ever seen a grizzly bear?" Nick asked Maggie.

"Lots of times." Her smile was distracted. Riding around the familiar territory was painful, more painful than she realized it would be. She was learning about a side of her personality she didn't know she possessed. When she was in New York, she was fully in New York. She had wondered how, after a few months of grieving while she lived with her aunt, she was suddenly able to marry Nick and move on with her life. Being back on the ranch answered that question. She had the capacity to compartmentalize her emotions. Whether it was healthy or not, she wasn't sure. All she knew was that being back at the ranch unleashed a well of emotions she hadn't yet dealt with, among them homesickness for all the long months she had been away, guilt for Mathew and for her family, and grief for the boy and the life she had lost.

She was drained and exhausted when they returned to the ranch. Nick darted furtive glances her way. She gave him a few unconvincing smiles and withdrew into her shell.

Over supper the family noticed the change in her. It was a sign of their growing trust in him that they turned to Nick for answers. He wished he had some to give. He had thought Maggie was healing and getting over things, but now she was once again the sad, grief-stricken girl he had first met. The difference being that she now clung to him like a lifeline. After supper they sat around the family room talking and laughing, all except Maggie who sat still and silent, and affixed to his side like she was welded to him.

"Maggie, what's wrong?" he asked as soon as they were upstairs and alone in their room.

In answer she drew him to her and kissed him. Despite the fact that it was a slow and tender kiss it ignited in him the usual flair of passion, so it took him a while to realize she was crying. Not until he tasted the salt of her tears on his tongue did he know. He pulled away from her and smoothed his hands over her cheeks.

"Maggie, please don't cry."

"It hurts so much," she stammered between sobs.

"I know, baby, I know." He rolled beside her and gathered her to him and he wasn't sure which hurt worse; watching her cry, or knowing she was crying for another man.

CHAPTER 27

The next morning Maggie was her old self once again, although Nick thought her smile looked forced. Then she kissed him and he forgot to care. Like all the other times they kissed, things spiraled beyond the point of reason. Heavy boot steps sounded in the hallway. Maggie froze and Nick groaned.

"Ten thousand acres and we can't get a moment alone," he said.

"Is a moment all it takes?" she asked with mock innocence.

He pounced and would have shown her, but there were voices in the hallway again, so he reluctantly let her go to get dressed.

"I'm making supper tonight," she announced at the breakfast table. He wasn't the only one who looked at her in surprise. "That's right, I learned to cook, and not only that but it's going to be an authentic Italian meal, complete with homemade ricotta cheese." She pronounced "ricotta" the way his mother did, and he smiled at her.

"What about homemade mozzarella?" He stressed the pronunciation on the last word to tease her.

"I don't have the proper ingredients for that, and if you tease me I won't let you be my helper," she said.

He shut up then, because nothing pleased him more right now than the thought of spending the day in the kitchen with his wife.

"This place is the size of my entire apartment," he said as he looked around the spacious kitchen.

"Our apartment," she amended. She stood on her toes to kiss him, and he didn't let her pull away.

"Why are you doing this?" he asked. By "this" she knew he meant putting on a happy face and cooking Italian food.

"Because I owe you much more than this. Because you stood beside me every day of the last seven months while I slowly learned how to live again, and because I can't stand to see the look in your eyes when you think I'm grieving over him."

"Aren't you grieving over him?" He searched her face to try and read her heart.

"Aren't you still grieving Dominic?" she asked. He had seen his best friend gunned down in the street only a few months before she saw Mathew killed.

The question caught him off guard. "Yes, I suppose, but it was different. I wasn't engaged to Dominic."

"I was engaged to Mathew, but he was also my best friend for all of my life. There's a lot to get over, and I'm sorry to say it's going to take some time, but, Nick, I didn't lie to you. You knew when you married me I was still in mourning."

"I know, Maggie. But I didn't know it would hurt so much to watch you grieve another man."

"I'm sorry," she said sincerely.

They were at an impasse, and he knew it. She was stuck in her grief, and he was stuck resenting it. He knew he was being unfair to her, but he loved her; the thought of her loving someone else was acutely painful to him, even if the other man had her first and was now gone. Her eyes filled with tears and he leaned down to kiss them away.

"Don't cry," he whispered. "We'll work it out."

She was so relieved by his proclamation her tears spilled over. "I'm so relieved," she told him.

"Why?" he asked. His hands smoothed up and down her waist.

"I don't want you to be sorry you married me. I don't want it to be over."

"Never," he said vehemently. "Never, Maggie, don't even think that. My family doesn't believe in divorce, and my faith won't allow it."

"Oh," she said. She stared at a spot on his chest to hide her disappointment.

"And I don't want it," he added. "I like being married to you."

She peered up at him, suddenly shy. "I like being married to you, too. Very much."

He tipped her face up and kissed her lightly, but they were interrupted by Will who entered the kitchen for a glass of water.

"It's like some sort of signal for your family to appear whenever I kiss you," he whispered when Will left the room.

She smiled against his lips. "It's probably for the best. I have a lot of work to do, and you know I'm not very good at organizing several different projects at once."

"I do know that," he said affectionately. "I'll help you," he said. He made her list all she planned to make, and kept her on track as she flitted from dish to dish. Supper was ready by their normal dinner time, and Maggie was more impressed than anyone.

"I couldn't have done it without Nick," she said and meant it.

"Good spouses make good partners," her father commented.

By the way Maggie beamed at him, Nick knew it was as close to a seal of approval as he was likely to get.

"How did you two happen together anyway?" he asked. Maggie couldn't believe the subject hadn't come up before, but she thought maybe her family was giving them space and trying to get to know Nick before pelting him with questions.

"I had to get her away from that horrible woman," Nick said. His clenched fists and clipped tone told them how much he had disliked Victoria.

"I see my sister-in-law is still her pleasant self," Matt remarked dryly. "Never met two people who were further apart in personality than your mother and her sister."

Nick gave Maggie an "I told you so" look, and she smiled. She was relieved to hear her mother and aunt were different from each other, but the other accusations Victoria had made against her father still weighed heavily on her mind

"So, when I saw how badly things were going between Maggie and her aunt. I asked her to move in with me," Nick continued.

Everyone sat forward and tensed on a collectively held breath.

"And my mother," he added hastily. "I guess I should have said that part first. Maggie slept on the couch."

The family leaned back in relaxed relief.

"And then I told him I couldn't stay," Maggie took over. "I knew I was being an inconvenience, so he proposed. Although I still don't understand why. I could have gotten my own apartment."

Now the family gave Nick a knowing, appreciative look. Maggie was as capable of living by herself as Libby's unborn child. They were suddenly ferociously glad this man had been there to look out for their Maggie.

To everyone's surprise, Anne volunteered to clean up the kitchen with Maggie. The oldest sister wasn't known for her domesticity.

"What did Victoria say to you when you lived with her?" Anne asked.

Maggie shrugged, unwilling to talk about it.

"Maggie," Anne said in the tone she had used when Maggie was little and unwilling to obey.

"She pushed me a lot to get a job and a future. She looked down on our life here. She said we were uneducated and backwoods-type people."

"What else?" Anne asked.

How does she do that, Maggie wondered. Her older sister could seemingly read her mind. "She said Mom died because of us. She said Dad didn't let her go to the doctor in time. She said he only wanted her to be a breeder." Her hands shook on the dish she was holding.

Anne stepped forward and took it from her hands. She pulled Maggie to her and hugged her tightly. "She lied, or she didn't know the truth. You were a little girl when Mom died, but I was twelve. I know exactly what happened. Mom was a little bit like all of us, but she had my stubbornness and Libby's untiring work ethic. Dad noticed her exhaustion and bugged her to go to the doctor, but she wouldn't. She said she was getting lazy in her old age. Finally one day he literally picked her up, put her in the truck, and drove her to the doctor. It's true that by the time they found the cancer it was too late, but it wasn't Dad's fault.

"And Mom was like you in her love of children. She wanted a dozen kids. Dad was the one who made her stop at four. He said if they had any more they were going to look like an orphanage." She pulled away and rested her hands on Maggie's shoulders so she could look into her eyes. "If there is one thing I want you to know about our parents, it's that they loved each other deeply. Mom and Dad were happy together. They had a great relationship, and we would all do well to imitate them. I might be a hard-nosed so and so to the rest of the world, but I love Will, and he knows it because I make sure of it. I put our relationship above everything else. You need to do the same with your husband, Maggie. I can see you grieving for Mathew, and that's okay, but Nick needs to know you love him. He needs to know he comes first, understand?" She chucked her under the chin and turned back to the dishes.

They finished the dishes in silence and joined the rest of the family in the living room. Maggie's mind was full of all Anne had told her. Nick had done everything in his power to take care of her and make her happy, and what had she given him in return? Nothing but sadness. She hurt him every time she thought of Mathew. She didn't know how he knew when she was grieving, but he did. It upset him, and no wonder. How would she feel if his friend Dominic had been a girl? Or if Angelina died and he mourned her?

She studied Nick as he talked to Kitty and Dante. He was wonderful and amazing, and she was holding him at arm's length. Well, no more. He was her husband, and from this night forward she would act like it—in every way.

"I'm tired," she announced suddenly.

"Me, too," Libby said. "I think we're going to head to bed. Night all."

"Goodnight," Maggie called absently. Nick had looked up at her when she made her proclamation, and he seemed to understand what she was trying to tell him because there was suddenly an intense heat bouncing between them.

They trudged up the stairs together and shared the bathroom while they washed their faces and brushed their teeth. When they reached the bedroom he kissed her slowly, tenderly, and with purpose. He wanted to know she was in her right mind when she gave herself to him. He wanted to know it was him she was giving herself to and not Mathew.

But then, like a purposely set back fire that explodes out of control, the passion between them once again flared. And then a heavy knock sounded on the bedroom door.

"You're kidding me," Nick mouthed.

Maggie laughed and covered his mouth with her hand, determined to get rid of whoever it was with expediency. "Yes," she said in as pleasant a tone as she could manage.

It was her father. "Libby's in labor. We're going to the hospital. Come on before Dobbie throws a saddle on his back and carries her there himself."

"All right," Maggie said shakily. Nick's lips were pressed against her neck doing something magical. She expelled a breath when he drew away.

"Notice how I'm not saying a word of protest or complaint," he said as he slid into his pants.

"Yes, why is that?" she asked.

"Because Will told me husbands work on a point system, and the more nice things you do for your wife, the more points she gives you."

Maggie could imagine Will saying something like that. "I have bad news for you."

His hand stilled on his shirt. "What?"

"You already have too many points for me to count. I'm afraid these new points are going to pile on top of all the others." She stood on her toes to kiss him and dodged his embrace when he reached for her. "Don't get started; I'm not sure Dad was joking about Dobbie."

CHAPTER 28

When they arrived in the yard with the rest of the family they learned Matt Chapman hadn't been exaggerating much about Dobbie's behavior. No one had ever seen the usually cool-headed cowboy in such a panicked tizzy before. He grabbed the keys to one of the family trucks, but Matt plucked them out of his hands.

"Oh, no you don't. I'm not having my daughter end up in a ditch somewhere because you drive like a fool. I'll drive you and Libby." He tossed the keys to Nick. "Nick will drive Maggie, and Dante will drive Kitty, Will and Anne in his car."

"But I can get us there faster," Dobbie protested.

"I can get us there alive," Matt said.

Libby groaned, bent over and clutched Dobbie's arm. "Stop arguing and let Dad drive," she panted. "I need you to hold me so I don't bounce."

The dirt road into town was notoriously bumpy and uncomfortable, even for someone who wasn't in labor.

"All right, Libby," Dobbie said tenderly.

They loaded into their respective vehicles. Maggie bobbed up and down on the seat until she noticed Nick's forlorn expression.

"I'm sorry we were interrupted again," she said. She rested her hand on his leg. "But you're going to be an uncle."

Her smile was contagious and he returned it. "I've never been an uncle before. It's sort of fun to have sisters."

"It's the best, although I've enjoyed meeting your five hundred cousins."

His expression turned wary. "I won't have to hold the baby, will I?"

"Not if you don't want to. Don't you like babies?"

"They're all right. I'm more comfortable with guns than newborns, I guess."

She smiled and looked out her window. Somewhere out there was Steve. The thought hit her anew and she shivered, wondering if he was watching them right now, waiting for his chance at her. Then again, maybe he wasn't there. Maybe he was still in New York. Had it really only been a few days ago that Victoria was beaten? Steve might still be there tailing her aunt, hoping to catch sight of the true object of his desire.

"What are you thinking?" Nick asked.

"The usual," she said.

"Baby, if I knew what you were usually thinking, I would have a lot more time on my hands because I could stop trying to figure it out."

"It's harder to be back here than I thought," she said. "The memories are fresh because I left as soon as it happened." She thought of him passing the location Dominic died on an almost daily basis, and she realized she had no idea what happened that day.

"Nick, what happened to Dominic?" Her tone was gentle. She turned to look at him with a soft, probing glance.

He inhaled sharply. He hated talking about it, hated thinking about it, but he couldn't expect her to heal if he wasn't willing to. "I already told you we were responding to a call together. My partner and I were getting off work, but when there's a call that big there's no going home. Dominic and his partner were starting for the day. We laughed when we saw each other. It was exhilarating to be on a big call together, sort of a dream come true, you know?" He glanced at her before turning back to the road. "There was a riot between two rival gangs outside of Chinatown. It was a freak thing, like a fight at a baseball game. Usually when they have face-offs like that it's a planned event, but that particular morning they both happened to be at the wrong place at the wrong time. Anyway, things were escalating out of control and the officer in charge called for more backup. After that everything happened at once. I had out my riot stick, but then we realized the firepower they had, and my partner told me to draw my weapon. I lost sight of Dominic for a second, and when he reappeared, one of the gang members had a bead on him. Everything stopped in that minute." He paused and swallowed. "I shot the guy, but it was too late. He had shot Dominic at point blank range."

She knew him well enough by now to know there was more he wasn't telling her. Her hand smoothed up and down his leg. "What else?"

"I think I might have hesitated." The words were so difficult for him to utter she knew he had never said them to anyone else.

"What makes you think that?" she asked.

"Everything stood still. It was a shock, seeing Dominic so blatantly in harm's way. My brain is sluggish when it comes to remembering the sequence of events, so I can't be sure, but it made me question myself. If I was too slow to save my best friend, what chance do strangers have with me as a protector?" His eyes shimmered with tears that didn't spill over.

She didn't attempt to placate him. She knew from experience it wouldn't work because she was working on her own mountain of guilt. A part of her wondered if she might have saved Mathew if she had done one thing differently. It was a tormenting game of "what if." Instead of offering words of comfort she scooted close and sat on her knees so she could lock her arms around his neck and give him a hug and a kiss on the cheek.

"Why did you get the medal?" she asked. She let him go and then sat back.

"Who told you about that? No, wait, let me guess—Alessa." He shook his head. "When I shot the guy who shot Dominic, he didn't go down. He seemed intent on taking out more cops, so I tackled him and wrestled the gun away from him."

A guy who tackled an armed assailant in the midst of a gang riot didn't sound like the same guy who would hesitate to shoot when his friend's life was at stake, but Nick would need to face his own demons in his own way.

Their procession arrived at the hospital. Dobbie carried Libby inside, despite the fact that she weighed fifty pounds more than usual. He had calmed down somewhat now that they were safely arrived, and his main goal became helping Libby through the process. The rest of the family trooped in behind the couple and waited in the lobby, all except Anne who was dispatched as the go-between in order to provide updates.

Two hours after their arrival at the hospital, Celia Grace Dobbins was born, weighing six pounds eight ounces. It took awhile for Libby and the baby to get cleaned up enough for the family to be able to visit, and then they passed her around tentatively, joyfully, while Dobbie fed Libby takeout food Will smuggled in for her.

"Do you want to hold her?" Maggie held out the tiny Celia for Nick. She wouldn't make him do it, but she knew he would like it after he conquered his fear. "I'll show you how."

"All right," he said. He tensed in concentration as he took the tiny bundle in his arms. Maggie peered over his shoulder.

"She's perfect," she said in an awed whisper.

"She is," he agreed in the same soft tone.

Maggie smiled at the picture they made, and for the first time when she pictured her future children they had Nick's dark eyes and hair. Somehow the thought wasn't painful; in fact it was pleasant, especially when she pictured them walking around the neighborhood and speaking with the same clipped accent as their father.

Nick turned and was frozen by the expression on her face.

"Ready to go home?" she asked.

He blinked and smiled at her as her meaning became clear. He nodded and handed the baby to Kitty, who was almost as uncomfortable with it as he had been. They said their goodbyes to the rest of the family who looked like they had no plans to leave any time soon. When they reached the car Maggie realized how tired she was. Her feet felt weighted, and her eyes started to droop.

"Go to sleep, sweetheart, I've got this," Nick told her.

"Are you sure? I don't want you to fall asleep driving."

"I'll be fine," he assured her. He held up the coffee he had purchased on their way out.

She smiled at him, lay down on the seat beside him, and rested her head on his leg. He smoothed his hand over her hair a few times.

"That feels good, and so familiar," she drowsed.

"That's because I do it every night when you can't sleep."

She rolled over slightly in order to see his face. "When can't I sleep?"

"Every night lately. You've been having nightmares."

"I have?" she asked. He nodded. The vision of herself twisting around in the bed, keeping him awake and then him soothing her back to sleep popped into her head, and she shivered at the emotion the picture evoked. He was always there for her, taking care of her, loving her. She owed him everything, and from now on she was going to give it. With that thought in mind she smiled, settled more comfortably in his lap, and fell asleep.

CHAPTER 29

Sometime later she was awakened when the truck jerked to an abrupt stop.

"It's all right," Nick said. "It's only an elk. I didn't hit it."

She sat up in confusion and watched the slow progress of the elk as it ambled in front of them. Her befuddled mind conjured the image of the last elk who walked in front of her as she rode in a truck on this same road. Everything about that day came slamming back into focus, and she started to scream.

"Maggie, what? What is it?" Nick asked. He shifted the car into park.

She put her hands over her mouth and tried to stop the screams, but she couldn't. Instead she shook her head furiously and removed her hands so she could gulp air. She had never told Nick the details of that day; she had simply told him Mathew was killed by Steve.

"What is it?" Nick tried again. He crept close and wrapped his arms around her.

"It was like this that day," she said. She didn't want to talk about it, but she owed him some explanation of her irrational behavior. "Steve had me in his truck and then the elk and I escaped and Mathew died in my arms." Her shudders wouldn't stop, even with Nick's comforting arms pressing her close.

"You were there? You watched it happen?" he asked. He had no idea she had been present during the events that took her fiancé. He only knew the stalker did it out of his mad pursuit of her. He had no idea she had been kidnapped or forced to watch. So much of her behavior started to make sense to him, especially her inability to move on and let go. She wasn't simply grieving; she was traumatized.

Her head bobbed against his shoulder. "It was my eighteenth birthday, right after Mathew proposed. I thought he would be safe, but he pursued us, and then Steve killed him. Because of me," she said, and then she started to weep. "Because of me. It's all my fault, all of it." The shameful truth was out now, but it did nothing to stem the flow of guilt. Mathew was dead, Victoria was beaten, and her family was in danger, all because of her.

Nick kept one arm firmly tucked around her. With the other he shifted into drive and continued home. This wasn't a discussion he wanted to have in the middle of the roadway, especially not when they were almost home anyway. Beside him Maggie continued to sob and tremble. His heart was anguished for her. He knew about guilt, irrational as it may be, and he also knew the power it could have over someone. They arrived home and he parked the truck once again.

He picked her up and carried her to their bedroom. He laid her softly on the bed and started to pull away in order to retrieve a cool washcloth for her forehead.

"Don't leave me," Maggie pleaded. "Please don't let me go." Both her arms were wrapped tightly around his neck in the same torturous position she used when she was asleep and having a nightmare.

"Never," he whispered, and his voice was gruff. "I'll never let you go, Maggie." He eased down beside her on the bed. Her eyes were closed, but her lips searched for his, and when they met they clung to him in the same way the rest of her body did.

Not like this, he thought. He tried in vain to turn off his brain and allow his body to take over, but he couldn't. He kept seeing Maggie's grief, so close and potent it was like a shroud. It was Mathew she wanted, not him.

"It can't happen like this," he said, pulling away from her.

Maggie sat up and blinked at him in confusion.

"I want it to be me," he continued in the same dull tone. "I want to know it's me you're with and not his ghost." He drew in a shaky breath. "You'll never be free of him, will you?" His Adam's apple bobbed as he swallowed convulsively.

"Nick," Maggie tried, but he withdrew from her and shook his head.

"Don't," he whispered hoarsely. "You don't have to apologize or explain. I knew how it was when I married you. I'm going to take a shower." When he turned, she caught the shimmer of tears in his eyes.

A flash of pain cut through her middle like the swipe of a knife. How could Nick believe she was thinking of Mathew when she was with him? Didn't he realize nothing was the same? No, of course he didn't because she had never told him. She had never explained to him, but how could she when she didn't understand it herself? He was right; a part of her was still attached to Mathew, and being back here reinforced that attachment. She had to do something, had to find closure, but what?

Suddenly she knew exactly what she had to do and where she had to go to lay Mathew's memory to rest. She swiped at her eyes and her hands came away wet. She hadn't realized she was crying because she felt numb and in shock. Nick's words had wounded her in a way she never would have expected because she felt his pain, and not her own. She had hurt him, and she had to make it right or die trying. She rose and then made her way to Kitty's room. She rummaged through Kitty's junk drawer until she found what she wanted, tucked the Swiss army knife into her pocket, grabbed a jacket, and headed outside.

Nick was already regretting his words to Maggie. He knew he had hurt her, and he hated that. He spoke from his own hurt and ruined the first real chance at intimacy between them. As soon as the hot spray of water hit his skin he knew it, and he also knew he needed to apologize to Maggie and make things right between them. He took a quick shower, wrapped a towel around his waist, and opened the door.

But the bed was empty. He called to her, but there was no answer. Far away he heard the click of the door downstairs and he froze. She wouldn't go outside by herself; she knew better. Did that lunatic have her?

He threw on his clothes with shaking fingers, not bothering to apply deodorant or comb his hair. When he dashed down the stairs and outside, Maggie was nowhere in sight. He looked around frantically and barely caught a glimpse of her blond head as it disappeared into the trees. She was running, and he took off after her at a sprint. What was she thinking going into the woods alone?

Maggie wasn't thinking; she was feeling, and what she felt was desperation. She had to fix things between her and Nick. She had to make it right. Her sleep-deprived, emotionally overloaded brain could only think of one way. Finally she arrived at her destination. When she saw the fort sitting forlorn and neglected, she stopped and sucked in a breath. She remembered Mathew kissing her, telling her he loved her, proposing to her, and showering her with roses. Her feet propelled her forward, even though she didn't want to go. Her hand reluctantly reached out to trace their initials.

"I loved you," she whispered. "I still love you, but I have to let you go. You'll always be a part of me, but you can't be the biggest part of me anymore. I'm sorry, sorry for everything." She choked on the last words. Momentarily her mission was forgotten as she put her hands over her face and broke down into tears, but then her resolve strengthened again. She took out Kitty's knife and started to carve, and as she did she talked to Mathew.

"You would like Nick," she told him. "He's sort of like all the cowboys we know, macho and protective. He even knows how to ride a horse, and he's funny. You guys would have been good friends." She smiled and swiped at her tears again. "Well, maybe not. You're both jealous and possessive. I miss you, Mathew. I miss your friendship as much as I miss anything. We could always talk about things, and you always knew where I was coming from. You always thought the best of me, and your opinion made me want to be who you thought I was. The sad truth is I'm not that great. I'm not smart or independent or brave, but with you none of that mattered, and that's how it is with Nick, too. He likes me despite all my weaknesses. Finding that twice in a lifetime is nearly a miracle, and I can't throw it away, even if it means I have to let you go." She paused and traced over their initials again. "I'll come back and visit here sometimes. I'll bring my kids, and I'll tell them about you, about all the time we spent here together."

When Nick stepped into the clearing the sight before him made his breath catch. Maggie knelt in front of a small building holding a switchblade. She was talking softly and crying, although she seemed oblivious to her tears.

"Maggie," he said gently, "put the knife down."

She jumped and whirled to look at him. "But I'm not finished."

Her tone was so puzzled he realized he had misunderstood her intentions, which made more sense. Despite her sadness, she had never seemed suicidal. "Finished with what?"

"Carving our initials." She held out her hand to him and he came forward. "We all carved our initials here, me and Mathew and my sisters and their boyfriends. Everything works out when you carve your initials here, so I'm adding ours."

He saw the beginning of his initials and hers lined up beside the ones Mathew had already carved. "You don't have to do this," he said.

"Yes, I do. I want to. I want things to work out between us, Nick. I want us to be happy."

"We are happy," he said.

"Are we? I know I am, but are you?"

"Yes," he said. He set aside the knife and pulled her into his embrace. "If all you can ever give me is a part of yourself, then it's enough, Maggie, it's *enough*. These last few months since I met you have been the best of my life. I didn't know it could be like this."

She stood on her toes to kiss him and as usual a fire erupted between them. She withdrew before it could get out of control. "There," she said. "That's what's different."

He smiled and pressed his face to her neck. "What are you talking about?" His tone was muffled because his lips were still pressed against her.

"It wasn't like this with Mathew. Kissing him was sweet and pleasant, but it didn't consume me the way kissing you does. I had no idea things could be so combustible between two people." She pushed him away from her because she wanted to look in his eyes. She cupped his face with her hands. "Don't you understand I could never confuse you and him?" She took a breath. "I loved Mathew, and it's difficult for me to say anything about him that might seem negative or disloyal, but I've had a lot of time to think about him and us. He and I lived in a bubble. Our relationship was untested. We never saw other people. We didn't work. Our families supported us. Mathew loved me, and that was his only ambition in life. We had happy dreams of having a family right away, but a part of me wonders about our future together. What really would have happened if I got pregnant at eighteen? Would his brother have started to resent having to do all the work on their ranch? Maybe it would have been all right, but it wasn't perfect, no matter how I made it seem. We both had our heads in the clouds, and eventually something would have made us fall to earth.

"But you are ambitious. You planned for your career as soon as you turned seventeen, and you've been working hard at it since then. I like that ambition. With you I learned things about myself, like the fact that I can hold a job and make it in one of the toughest cities in the world. You and I are living in the real world, and we're thriving together." She pressed her palm to his chest.

"This morning," he began.

"I was with you, and I knew it. I wasn't pretending you were Mathew. I wasn't thinking about him. I purposed to be with you because I wanted to be with you. I still want to be with you."

He smiled, his relief palpable. If Maggie was telling the truth, then he wasn't some pale replacement of her former love. She truly wanted to be with him. "I want that, too." He kissed her and she melted into his embrace. His heart was near to bursting with happiness and hope for their future. "Maggie, I lo…" At first he didn't understand where the sharp pain came from or why he couldn't complete his sentence, and then everything went black and he slumped to the forest floor.

CHAPTER 30

"I knew you'd come back to me."

It was like before, Maggie thought, except now Steve stood over *Nick's* unconscious body. But it would end the same, she had no doubt. Somehow, someway he would kill Nick. She would watch it happen, and she would go insane. And this time it would be worse because she was directly responsible. She knew about the risk and she ran into the woods anyway.

"Come on," Steve said. He held out his hand to her.

Something within her snapped. Not this time. It wouldn't be the same, no matter what she had to do. If Nick was going to die, then she was going to die with him. "No," she said. She crossed her arms over her chest and stood up to her full height.

Steve looked down at Nick's prone figure. "Come with me now, or I'll kill him."

Maggie uncrossed her arms and curled her hands into fists. "You'll touch him over my dead body," she hissed, and then she leapt.

The surprise knocked Steve backward, but the force wasn't enough to knock him to the ground. The sound he made was laughter, and when Maggie heard it her rage increased. How dare he laugh at her? He had taken away her fiancé, scared her family, beaten her aunt, and knocked her husband unconscious, and now he was laughing at her? She kneed his groin as hard as she could and then he did fall to the ground. She didn't stop, though, she couldn't. She kicked him and kicked him as he lay on the ground. She was glad she was wearing her cowboy boots with the hard, pointed toes.

When he rallied from the groin kick she knew she would be in trouble, and it happened sooner than she would have thought. One hand shot out to grab her ankle then she was lying on the forest floor beside him, and he was advancing on her.

"I don't like disobedience in a wife, Maggie," Steve said menacingly.

"I'm not your wife," she screamed.

He climbed on top of her and grabbed her arms to pin them above her head. She writhed beneath him, but he groaned and smiled.

"Oh, that feels so good," he said.

For a moment she thought she might throw up. Her frantic fighting was turning him on, and the thought sickened her as nothing else. By the evil, lecherous look on his face she began to fear for more than her life; she began to fear for her virtue. If she didn't get away from him, he would most likely have his way with her. Her head twisted to the side and she caught his arm in her teeth. She bit until she tasted blood, but she didn't release her hold. When she withdrew her mouth she had a piece of his flesh between her teeth. She spit it out and bounded away from him when he howled in pain.

"You're not my Maggie," he yelled. She had barely run five steps when he caught her by the hair and turned her to face him. His arm was trailing blood, and so was his lip.

"I've never been yours," she yelled at him. "I don't belong to you. I belong to Nick. He's my husband, and I love him. You're sick."

"My Maggie would never have talked to me that way. You're an impostor! What have you done with her?" He shook her shoulders until her teeth rattled. She fought him, but it was useless. He held her in a viselike grip. "I'll kill you. I'll kill him. I'll kill them all until I find her."

That statement gave her the surge of strength she needed to break away from him. She kneed his groin again, but he was too far gone in his rage to feel it. Now instead of trying to hold her, he was fighting her. They hit each other wherever they could land blows. She knew hers were ineffective jabs, but every time he hit her it was like a piece of granite connecting with her skull. Soon she would lose consciousness, and then he would kill her. And Nick. And her family. That thought alone kept her upright, and so she kept fighting.

"Maggie, drop."

Even in the midst of her panic and anger she knew Nick's voice. She heard the command and didn't hesitate to follow it. A second after she dropped to the ground the shot sounded. She rolled onto her stomach and saw Nick sitting up, dazed, but aiming the gun levelly. Her head swiveled around to see Steve with a hole in his chest. Amazingly that didn't stop him. He advanced on Nick who shot him again, and again, and again. Finally on the fourth shot Steve fell to the ground, face down. Nick eased to a standing position and kept the weapon trained on the still form in front of him. Maggie was glad. She didn't trust Steve not to be biding his time. The vision of him suddenly springing up and attacking again wouldn't go away.

Nick must have had the same thought because he stayed put and didn't move forward to check for a pulse. "I'm going to stay here. Run back to the house and call the sheriff."

She hesitated, unwilling to leave him. A part of her was afraid he wouldn't be there when she returned. The unconscious madman had a history of taking the people she loved.

"It's all right, baby," Nick said, reading her mind. "I'm not going anywhere."

She nodded, turned, and sprinted back to the house. When she arrived, her father, Kitty, Dante, Will, and Anne were home and frantically searching for her and Nick. Anne screamed at the sight of her and a part of Maggie's brain registered the fact that she had never heard her sister scream before.

"It's all right," Maggie said. "Steve attacked us, but Nick shot him. They're in the woods by the fort. Can you call the sheriff? I don't want to leave them alone out there." She turned to go, but her father caught her.

"Whoa, little girl. You're not going back there."

"But Dad, I have to. He might still be alive. I need to check on Nick and make sure he's all right." She tugged her arm but her father's grip was relentless.

"I'll go check on him, and I'll take my gun," her father said.

"I'll go, too," Kitty said.

"Not without me," Dante said.

"I'll wait for the sheriff and direct him to the location," Will said.

"Come on, sweetie," Anne said. She put an arm around Maggie and led her inside. "Let's get you cleaned up. Whose blood is on you?"

Maggie looked down at herself for the first time. She was a gruesome sight with smears and trails of blood all over her. "A little of everyone's, I think."

Anne led her upstairs to the room she and Nick were sharing. Maggie glanced at the bed and blushed, hoping Anne didn't notice the tangle it was in. Had it really only been a few hours ago they arrived home from the hospital?

"I'll make you some tea while you shower," Anne said.

Maggie nodded. It was different having Anne care for her. Libby was the nurturer who took over after their mother died. Anne had been the tough disciplinarian, but her tenderness wasn't altogether surprising. Marrying Will had a softening effect on her sister, and now everyone knew her tough woman act was a façade.

She took a long shower and washed her body and hair three times before she began to feel clean. She put on Nick's t-shirt and flannel pants, even though they were sizes too big for her. She wanted their comfort right now. When she exited the bathroom, Anne held the sheet back for her and she climbed into bed. Anne perched on the edge of the bed and stroked her hair in the comforting way Nick did while Maggie sipped at the hot tea.

"You surprise me, little sister," Anne said.

Maggie smiled faintly. "I don't imagine myself being able to surprise anyone."

"I think you've surprised us all. We've all thought of you as the baby, as the soft and sweet little girl who needs our protection, but in the last few months you have survived two attacks by a stalker, lost your best friend and fiancé, moved half the world away, married a stranger, and made a new life for yourself. I think we've been wrong about you. I think you're the strongest one of us."

Maggie's smile grew. She certainly didn't think of herself that way, but it was nice to hear, especially from her oldest and toughest sister. Fatigue was catching up with her though, and she barely managed to whisper, "Love you, Anne," before she fell into a dreamless sleep.

When she woke, it was dark out, and Nick was there. For a while they looked at each other, and then she was in his arms and they were kissing.

"I thought I was going to lose you," she said. She pulled back so she could smooth her hands over his cheeks.

"I told you I won't leave you, Maggie." He kissed her again, and then broke off to talk to her. "You should have run away."

"I couldn't leave you. He would have killed you for sure if you followed us."

"He could have killed you," Nick said. "He almost did." He shuddered and pulled her against his chest.

"If you were going to die, I wanted to die, too. I don't want to go on without you, Nick." She wrapped her arms around his waist and tried to weld herself to him.

Nick swallowed convulsively. "You told him you love me; did you mean it?"

"Don't you know, Nicky? How could you not?"

"You were in love with him, and you were grieving. I didn't think you had room for me in your heart."

She eased away again so she could look into his eyes. "But I do. I love you, Nick. I never expected to love again after Mathew, especially not so soon after, but you have been my light in the darkness. You have cared for me and protected me and loved me from the moment I met you."

"What?" he asked. His heart was thudding heavily in his ears. She loved him. He couldn't believe it.

"Do you love me? You've never actually said." Her eyes dropped to his chest. She knew he loved her, but that didn't mean he was in love with her. He might simply see her as a friend.

He laughed and that brought her attention back to his face. "Sweetheart, do you really think I would give up my bachelorhood for anything less than absolute devotion? Maggie, I fell in love with you the moment I saw you sitting on that park bench. I've never looked back, and I've never regretted a moment of our time together."

She pressed her face to his neck and rained happy tears down the front of his shirt. "Is it over? Is he really gone?"

"Yes. The coroner pronounced him dead. It's over, Maggie. Forever."

She gripped his shirt and her tears started anew. "I'm so relieved. I feel like I can breathe again."

They lay in silence for a few minutes, enjoying the peace and relief in the moment.

"Maggie, did you mean what you said about it being all right if I left my job at the park?"

She looked up into his face again to read his eyes. "You want to go back to the fifth precinct?"

He focused on a spot behind her, thinking. "In that moment, when I came to and realized he was hitting you, there was no hesitation. I knew what needed to be done to save you. All my old instincts came back to life, and I felt alive again for the first time since I left my old job. But, no, I wasn't thinking of the fifth precinct." He took a breath and forced a smile. "The sheriff offered me a job here. They're looking for a new deputy."

Her mouth fell open in shock. "You would leave Brooklyn?"

He looked into her eyes then and ran a finger down her cheek. "This is your home. Your family is here. You're a part of this place."

"I'm a part of you," she told him. "And I want to go home. To our home in Bensonhurst, only do you think some day we might be able to get our own apartment?"

"What about our own house?"

"What?"

"When my dad died his life insurance premium paid off my mom's apartment. For the last few years I've been saving almost all my money in order to be able to afford a house. With what you've earned from your job, it put us over the top for a down payment."

"A house," she said dreamily. "A house of our very own. Do you think maybe we could buy something in the neighborhood? I would hate to move too far from your mom, Mrs. Esposito, and the DeLucas."

"We'll live anywhere you want, go anywhere you want, do anything you want. Say the word and it's yours," he promised.

"Right now I don't want to be anywhere but here with you," she said and put her face up to be kissed.

A few years later Edda made the journey to Montana with them. She had never left Brooklyn before, and had no idea how easily she would fall in love with the land, or how easily she would fall in love with Matt Chapman. The two were married at the end of the visit, and she never left Montana again. At the reception, Nick jokingly thanked her for making his wife his sister, but everyone was happy to see the two so happy with each other. Edda's soft side brought out Matt's tender nature, but her tough-as-nails Brooklyn upbringing kept him on his toes, too.

When they returned to Brooklyn, Nick went back to his old job at the fifth precinct. Maggie worried about him on an almost daily basis, but she knew he was good at his job, and that thought gave her courage during the long nights he was away. Eventually he moved up to dayshift and her fears eased, and then evaporated completely. They remained in Bensonhurst a few more years until their children entered school, and then they decided to move near their family. They returned to Montana and built a house on a small tract of land Matt gave them as a wedding present. By that time they had a son and daughter. After the move they had twins—a boy and a girl. Maggie stayed home with the kids whenever she wasn't helping her father and

Dobbie on the ranch. Nick became a sheriff's deputy and worked nights again for a few years until he worked his way up to dayshift once more.

Libby and Dobbie had three more children after Celia, all girls. Maggie and Libby took turns driving their children to and from school every day.

Anne became a prosecutor in nearby Billings. She and Will had three boys. Will stayed home with the children and worked as a freelance writer and editor for a popular sporting magazine.

Kitty and Dante were the only family members who lived outside Montana. They remained in Omaha, Nebraska. Kitty eventually became an FBI agent while Dante stayed an actuary. When they were unable to have children of their own, they adopted a brother and sister from foster care. They were half-Hispanic and most people assumed they were biological children because of Dante's Spanish heritage.

Every summer a handful of Nick's cousins came for a visit, and occasionally one of them found work and stayed. After a few years rumors started to circulate that the Marinos were part of a mob relocation program. Maggie was furious, but Nick and his cousins found it amusing and took it in stride, even occasionally laying on their thick Brooklyn accent whenever a cocky cowboy became unruly with them.

Eventually the family reunited with the Henshaws again for their yearly July fourth celebration. At first Lydia Henshaw found it painful to watch Maggie and Nick together, but when their children began calling her Grandma Lydia, she accepted the situation, along with her role as surrogate grandmother.

Nick returned to the fort where so much had happened and finished carving his initials and Maggie's in the wall. Every year he checked the small building and shored up whatever was sagging so that by the time his children were old enough to play with it a few boards had been replaced, but it was still in good condition.

The first time her kids discovered the place they took Maggie by the hand and led her there. The memories were as potent to her as they were when they happened, but the good times outweighed the bad, and she smiled. Some day she would tell her children the truth of what transpired there, and about the man who came before their father, but on this day she smiled as she showed them the initials carved in the wall.

"Why are they carved there?" her oldest son asked.

"Because this place is magic," she said. She ran her finger over the initials and smiled again.

Thank you for reading *Cowgirl on the Run,* the 4th book in the Queens of Montana Series. For more books, please check out my website at www.vanessagraybartal.com